WICKED IN MY BED

TAMARA

COPYRIGHT

CHAPTER
ONE

London 1816

Daphne stood before the mirror at Madame Laurent's modiste and adjusted the bodice of her wedding gown. She glanced down at her bosom, not the largest by any means. In fact, she probably was a good handful at best, but still, at least she had a little to fill out the elaborate embroidery Madame Laurent had stitched for her.

"You look absolutely lovely, Daph," her closest friend Ashley Woodville, now the Duchess of Blackhaven, said from a nearby settee.

Daphne met her friend's gaze in the mirror and smiled. "I'm so happy to be here with you, for some weeks at least."

"And your betrothed, what is he like? He's the vicar at Grafton, I understand. Mama wrote and told me Mr. Bagshaw had left his position, which I must say I was quite surprised by."

"Oh yes, well, his wife ran off with the baker's boy, and he could not bear to stay in the village where everyone knew what had happened. All scandalous, but Mr. Bagshaw did not deserve such treatment, even though he was a terrible bore."

Ashley chuckled, rubbing her stomach, which was showing the first roundness of a child.

Daphne took a deep breath, knowing she had to tell her friend the truth before another day passed. She stepped from before the mirror and joined her on the settee. "There is something I must admit to, but please do not judge me."

Ashley took her hands and squeezed them. "I would never judge you. You must know that."

Daphne hoped that was the case, but even so, nerves fluttered in her belly at admitting the truth. "Regarding my betrothed, well, we're not technically betrothed yet. I wish for him to propose to me. He would certainly make the most perfect husband. He is handsome and with a good living, and resides in Grafton. Perfect for my happiness, and he is not forceful or demanding, which I do not want in a husband."

Ashley stared at her for several moments before she frowned. "So ... you're not betrothed? Why are you in London buying a wedding gown, new undergarments, and unmentionables if you're not engaged, Daph?"

Daphne shrugged, slumping back into the cushions on the settee in the most unladylike manner. She stared at several other young ladies looking at material across the store and tried not to recoil at their high-pitched squeals when they came across something to their liking.

"I have been hoping he would ask, and I do believe he's on the cusp of doing so. He merely needs a little push."

"A push?" Ashley repeated. "How can you push him if you're in London and he's in Grafton, pray tell?"

"Well, my thinking is that he will miss me while I'm

gone, and as I have friends here in town and my very best friend is a duchess, well, that will make him even more determined to marry me when he's told all of this on Sunday's service. Mrs. Bennet will tell him. You know how much she loves gossip, and I was sure to drop into her ear where I was going. I think he will miss me while I'm gone. I normally help with the children on Sunday, teaching them letters and numbers you see, and I'll not be there. My plan is faultless. He may even travel to London to find me."

Ashley gaped, her eyes wide, and at her continual silence, Daphne fought not to cringe. Was her plan not a good one? Did her friend think she was mad? She possibly was, but at nine and twenty, it was past time to think of what she could do to find a husband and act instead. If she did not marry soon, she would be an even older maid and never have a child, and she desperately wanted a daughter or son of her own.

"So you're not engaged?" Ashley stated again.

"No, I'm not. But that does not mean I cannot be organized and prepared and order my wedding gown while I'm in London. It will mean that I can return to Grafton ready to wed within a month of the vicar asking me, and we may start our family immediately. You know how much I want to be a mama. I see how happy you are with Blackhaven, and I'm sometimes overcome with longing for the same. Please do not judge me, Ash. I could not bear it from you."

"Oh, Daph," she said, pulling her into a tight hug. "I will never judge you. I love you like a sister, and I think it's marvelous you're being so prepared. You'll have everything ready as soon as the vicar corrects his priorities and asks for your hand in marriage. I think it's most forward-thinking of you."

Daphne nodded. "I could not agree more," she said.

"Now, let us finish hemming this gown, and then we shall go to Gunter's for tea. I think we've earned it after our shopping sojourn."

"Sounds perfect indeed," Ashley returned.

Corey, the Duke of Renford, sat within a secluded corner of Whites. After a night carousing London, he sipped his whisky, the amber liquid soothing his muscles, and mind.

The city was a welcome reprieve from Europe, where he had spent the majority of the past five years. Not that anyone knew of his spying for the British army, and nor would they ever, but now the war was over. England had won, and Napoleon had lost. A time to celebrate, to enjoy what London had to offer, and he would indulge his many appetites and not feel the slightest guilt over the fact.

Feminine laughter caught his attention from the bowed window, and he glanced outside and spied the Duchess of Blackhaven in deep discussion with another lady he had never seen before. The lady covered her mouth when she laughed as if she were embarrassed by doing so.

She was a pretty piece, tall and slim, with not a lot of breast, unfortunately. He sighed, clearing his throat as he watched them. The Duke of Blackhaven's carriage rolled to a stop, and Blackhaven opened the door for them, clearly in this part of town to collect them. The duke jumped to the ground and kissed his wife, not caring who saw before bussing the other lady's cheeks.

He supposed being back in London, and with the Season gaining momentum, there would be many ladies, such as the one he just viewed in town, searching for a husband, a love match that so many women craved. Not that he was interested in such unions.

He needed a mistress above anything else and would have one secured before the end of the Season. His life was complicated enough, and he did not need a wife, making it even more so.

"Renford!" The bellowing of his name made him start.

He turned to find Viscount Billington striding toward him, arms outstretched. "Damn, my good friend, it is pleasing to see you. I was not sure you would return this Season, but I'm glad to see that you have."

Renford stood and allowed Billington—his closest friend and one he had not seen for some time—to hug him. Working for the British army meant he had traveled at a day's notice sometimes. One moment he was in London, the next, Spain or France, wherever the Duke of York needed him.

But there would be no more missives in the middle of the night sending him on any more assignments. He was home now. Able to submit to whatever he wished. And he wanted to indulge a lot.

"Billington," he said, smiling. "I'm pleased to see you. Come, have a drink with me."

Billington waved over a footman and ordered two new whiskies. "I'm glad that Grand Oaks has not kept you away this year. What are your plans for the Season? We're to host a ball Thursday next. I will send an invitation this afternoon, and you must attend."

Corey laughed, having missed his friend for the many years he had worked for the army. In fact, he missed many things with his sporadic, mysterious lifestyle. The quiet of the countryside, honesty from his countrymen, living without danger or intrigue that wanted to sneak up on you

TAMARA GILL

at any moment. As the Duke of Renford, he was also not humble enough not to admit he enjoyed life's luxuries bestowed upon him in his position. And the women. He missed the fairer sex most of all, and he would ensure he had his fill of them before leaving town.

"No, everything is as it should be at the estate, and I'm here for the Season. I shall, of course, attend your ball." He thanked the footman and finished his whisky. "Although I'm off this evening to Dame Plaisir's masque. Do you remember the fun we've had at those?" he asked Billington. Knowing it would be years before he forgot the many sinful nights.

Billington groaned and slumped back in his chair. "Of course I remember those balls, but they're no longer for me. But I wish you well if you're attending. I'm certain you'll have a *pleasurable* night," he taunted.

Corey nodded, knowing he would. "I'm happy to see you're settled and married. You must introduce me to your wife. I've yet to meet the woman who brought my debauched friend to the aisle."

A look of pure bliss crossed Billington's visage, and Corey was happy for him. For some time, he did not think Billington would ever marry, and he was happy his friend had found a woman he loved.

"You will adore Lila. She is my life now," he admitted.

Corey could well believe that. "As I'm sure you are hers," he answered. "But I cannot say that I shall not miss you at Dame Plaisir's this evening, but I'm certain that I shall enjoy myself, even if you're not there."

Billington shook his head, his eyes alight with mischief. "Still the cad, I see." He paused, studying him a moment. "I gather then you're not looking for a wife?"

"Not at all," Corey admitted, knowing his friend would

6

not take this conversation further. "A mistress, yes, but wife, no thank you."

"A mistress, hmm." Billington narrowed his eyes. "I shall have to leave that search up to you too, my friend. I'm long past those expenses."

"I'm glad that you are." He cleared his throat, folding the paper he held in his lap, and threw it onto the table before them. "But I shall give you a full account of my success. No harm in that."

Billington chuckled. "No harm at all."

TWO

Daphne handed the silver-embossed invitation to the carriage driver and waited while he studied the address.

"Are you certain, Miss Raven, that this is where you're to attend this evening?" he asked her, the deep frown of concern wedged between his eyes.

Daphne looked over at the invitation and nodded. "I'm certain. That is the invitation the Duchess of Blackhaven had her maid deliver to me this evening. Viscountess Leigh is to meet me there as my chaperone. I'm certain the duchess is not wrong," she said, hoping the old retainer would not argue the fact any longer and certainly not out on the street before everyone who lived on the square.

"Maybe we ought to check with Her Grace?" he suggested.

Daphne shook her head, not willing to do such a thing. "The Duchess is indisposed this evening and is not to be disturbed. I'm certain this is the correct ball." Daphne stepped toward the carriage and climbed up inside without waiting for a footman to help her.

She settled her honeyed-silk gown about her legs and checked that her black mask with gold embellishments of feathers and little faux jewels was secure.

This evening's ball was sure to be a feast for one's eyes. A masque, and one Ashley had said was held yearly at Lady Owen's London home.

Why her driver was acting all uncertain, she could not understand. All would be well. Ashley would not steer her into anything untoward.

The carriage door closed, and she was soon rolling along toward the ball. The streets of Mayfair were busy with night revelries, people going all over the city for their respective outings.

Butterflies took flight in her stomach at seeing Viscountess Leigh once again. It had been years since she had seen Ashley's older sister, and she hoped they would be able to slip into the easy comradery they had always had.

The carriage rolled to a halt within a few minutes before a grand town house she did not recognize. Daphne looked out of the carriage window, studying the home. Where she thought to see numerous windows lit from the entertainment inside, nothing but drawn curtains and black glass glistened back. The city lanterns were all that greeted her.

And yet, numerous people made their way up the front steps of the house, their gowns as grand as the one she'd borrowed from Ashley, their faces covered with masks.

The carriage door opened, and the driver held out his hand. Daphne placed her hand in his, smiling at the servant's unease. "Do not look so worried. This is the correct address. All will be well. I'm certain of it." Daphne started toward the front steps before stopping and turning about. "Oh, and Lady Leigh will return me home. No need to wait," she said, giving the driver one last wave before leaving him standing and watching after her like a concerned parent.

Daphne walked into the home, handing her cloak to a waiting footman before following the crowd into a ballroom. The room was unlike anything she had ever seen before. Although new to town, she had read many accounts from Ashley regarding her outings and had been able to imagine many of the events merely from her friend's words. But this ballroom was not what she expected.

There were very few candles, and the room was cloaked in shadows and mystery. And while the music was lively and played from a floor above, you could not see them at all. Rows and rows of black silk hung across the ceiling space, just above the candles, which did not look safe at all. One good draft and the house would go up in flames for certain.

She looked about the room, searching for Lady Leigh. She was supposed to be dressed in a blue silk gown and silver peacock mask, and yet everyone seemed to be dressed similarly to her. All gold and black, no blue gowns at all.

"And who may you be, beautiful?" a deep baritone whispered in her ear, making her start.

She turned to face the gentleman wearing a mask over one eye. Was it for show or practical reasons? "Is that your mask, my lord, or have you lost your vision in your eye?" she asked, not wanting to assume one way or another, nor wishing to cause offense.

He grinned, lifting the singular piece of leather, revealing a dark-brown eye that matched his other.

They sparkled in mischief, and something in the way he looked at Daphne made her heart skip a beat.

"It is only for show." His gaze dipped to her lips and

then farther along her body, leaving her skin to prickle with awareness. She opened her fan and waved it before her face.

Who was this forward gentleman?

"Do you always look at women you have just met as if you wish to eat them, my lord?" she asked, hoping that she did not insult him with her use of honorifics or lack thereof. For all she knew, he could be a common man or a prince. Not that he should have come up to her at all and started speaking to her. That was not the way introductions worked in the upper echelons of society.

"Only the women whom I'm interested in eating," he quipped, his lips twisting into a wicked grin.

Daphne did not know how to respond. Never in her life had she been spoken to in such a way. Not that she knew what he meant, but by the way he looked at her, hunger burning in his eyes, she could only imagine.

She glanced about the room as a sense of dread settled over her. There was something wrong about this ball, and yet she could not pin what that was.

"And so I can assume from your conversation with me that I'm a lady you wish to eat?" she asked, completely lost as to what they were talking about and why. Never in her life had she ever had such an absurd interaction with another person, not to mention a man.

He chuckled, sipping a beer she had not seen him holding. "Will you dance with me?" he asked her, holding out his hand and finishing his beer at the same time before handing off his glass to a passing footman.

His question gave her a little sense of relief. A dance was common for balls, and she could do that easily enough, even though he had yet to tell her who he was.

He reached for her hand, escorting her toward where

11

other couples prepared to dance before the first notes of a waltz floated through the room.

Without warning, he stepped close, and the scent of sandalwood and sin teased her senses. She fought not to breathe deep his intoxicating fragrance and concentrated instead on the dance. She had not waltzed for many years, and only then at a country dance in the Grafton Hall.

His large hand settled low on her back, his other encasing hers at their side. Daphne looked up at the man and found him watching her.

"You're so beautiful," he whispered. "I do not believe we've ever met, and yet I feel as though we have," he said as if he were trying to muddle through his thoughts.

Daphne was certain she had never met him before in her life. She would have remembered had she done so. No one forgot an Adonis, and one who seemed determined to flirt with her, even when he did not know who she was or where she was from. He was so muscular, so tall, and made her long-meg stature feel petite for the first time in her life.

The waltz started to play, and he swept her into the dance. Daphne inwardly sighed at being held by the assertive man who knew how to dance.

The poor Grafton vicar was no dancer at all. In fact, she could not remember the last he had danced with her. Certainly, he did not at the previous Grafton ball.

Daphne met the stranger's eyes and found him watching her. "I'm—"

"No names, we do not need such trivial introductions this evening, but before the night ends, and if it pleases you, we can remove our masks and declare ourselves."

"We will?" she asked, curious. "Are you hiding who you are from me? Is there something about you that you do not like others to know?" She watched him.

His eyes narrowed before he shook his head, dismissing her words. "Nothing of the kind, but when we have mystery between us, life can be so much more freeing."

Daphne raised her brows, unsure what that meant either, but willing to play his game. She could remain anonymous for at least a few hours before returning home.

"So what shall we call each other then?" she asked. "Since we're not able to use our real names."

He leaned close, the breath of his words teasing her ear. "You may call me Wicked, and I shall call you Virtuous. You appear so angelic, even though I know that cannot be the case. You would not be here otherwise."

His words made little sense, and when about to question him on them, she caught sight over his shoulder of a couple in a darkened corner of the room. They were seated on a daybed, but it was what they were doing on the daybed that made her mouth gape. "Oh my," she said, causing several couples to turn in their direction.

Her gentleman friend, Wicked or whoever he was, grinned at the people she had spied. "They appear to be having a lot of fun. Would you care to slip away and have some fun of our own?"

Daphne gaped at him before closing her mouth with a snap. Have some of their own? What kind of party had Ashley allowed her to attend?

Looking about the room, she studied more of the guests and realized why the carriage driver questioned her destination. She questioned where she was now too.

This was no ball. This was a brothel.

THREE

N ever in his life had Corey been so enamored by a woman he did not know. And not only that but a woman he had not seen in her entirety. Her pretty nose sat beneath a silk mask, her eyes wide and bright looked about the room with interest and, if he were any judge, a little trepidation.

A modest whore. Whoever had heard of one. Certainly not him.

Was this the first masked ball of this kind she had ever attended? The idea that she was a virgin to such entertainment left him even more intrigued.

"I'm gathering from your startled expression that you've never been to one of these balls before." He took her hand, placing it on his arm, and guided her around the edge of the ballroom floor. He would dance again with her later. First, he needed her to relax and enjoy her surroundings.

She shook her head, and he patted her hand, hoping it would calm her nerves. "Well, you are not in any danger. No one will force themselves on you here. This ball is for gaiety and to let one forget the world's problems for one night at least."

She glanced up at him, and he had the distinct impression she had caught something in his voice he was normally very careful to disguise. The world, as far as he knew it, was a dangerous and cruel place. Certainly not for the faint of heart, not that he wanted the pretty little chit on his arm to ever come to that realization.

"Is that why you're here this evening, my lord? To escape your life?" she asked him.

He harrumphed, supposing he had. Since he was no longer working for the British army and was able to live out the remaining days of his life as a rich, titled gentleman, a ball such as the one they were attending was just the tincture he required to forget.

And mayhap have a good night's sleep if he drowned himself in enough wine.

"In some way, I suppose I am," he answered her. "To be completely honest with you, my virtuous beauty, I'm searching for a mistress."

He felt her startled intake of breath and was delighted at how innocent she was. But no one who attended such a ball was in truth. Was this part of her attraction? How she lured men such as himself to her side? The thought of bedding a woman who did not have a list of lovers as long as his arm did have its appeal. No one wanted to end up with the pox.

"A mistress?" she all but squeaked. "Well, I'm sorry to disappoint you, my lord, but I'm not the woman you ought to be squandering your time with. I'm not looking for a lover," she said, her cheeks turning a delightful rosy hue.

He grinned, hoping he could change her mind about that fact. "Tell me who broke your heart, and I shall end him. And then, if you're willing, I shall make yours whole again, but only if you choose to be mine."

And he wanted her to be his. Her body moved in her silk gown like a goddess. A woman who knew how to use her womanly curves and delectable form to seduce a man without any words spoken. And tall. Delightfully tall, so that she felt perfectly in proportion to him.

His stomach clenched in need, and he took a calming breath. He needed to tread carefully. The last thing he wished to do was spook the woman, and he could not let her go without learning her name. After this night, he may never see her again, and that in itself would be a tragedy.

"I have never had my heart broken, my lord. Whatever makes you think that I have?" she asked.

They walked past four couples copulating, their only privacy in a darkened part of the ballroom was transparent silk curtains, which were no seclusion at all.

"Oh my," she said at his side.

He paused to watch the four guests and couldn't help but bite back a grin at their antics.

"Is this what you had in mind for yourself when you came to this ball?" she asked him, meeting his gaze.

He stared at her, unsure how to answer. While he had never been one for voyeurism, he could not deny that watching others make a beast with two backs wasn't amusing and did give him a hard cock. How could it not? Was there anything more sensual and arousing than a woman taking pleasure?

"I prefer a private room, and while I did come here searching for a mistress, you have gained my attention now. Not," he went on when she blanched at his words, "that I expect anything from you. I merely wish to get to know you better and learn your name."

"Well," she huffed, moving them along the side of the room and away from the rutting foursome. "I will not be telling you my name, and nor will you get to know me at all. I think I need to be honest with you, my lord, so you will understand the reasoning behind my statement."

"Go on," he said, curious, while also enjoying how her mouth moved when she spoke. Her lips were pouty and soft-looking. Perfect for kissing in dark corners and abandoned terraces.

"Well, I think I have come to this ball by mistake. I was supposed to be at Lady Owen's masked ball, but I do not believe this is what my friend had in mind when her maid delivered her invitation."

Dread pooled in Corey's stomach, and he frowned. The chit had a maid? A friend who had been invited to one of London's most highly sought-after masked balls. That invitation list was exclusive, if ever there was one. Not that he had not also been invited, but this ball had more appeal than a gaggle of unmarried debutantes searching for a husband.

"You must have friends with means then, my virtuous beauty. Care to tell me who they are?" he asked, trying to keep the panic from entering his voice.

"No, I could never do that. I do not know you or if I can trust you, my lord. For that matter, I do not even know if you're a lord at all or a man of trade or a chimney sweep."

Corey laughed, having never had anyone state such an absurd thing to him. "I can assure you I'm no chimney sweep."

"Even so," she continued. "To tell you the truth puts me in your power and my friends too, and I will not do that. Not even for a handsome face like yours."

"Mmmm, so you think I'm handsome?" he teased. "I

think you're one of the prettiest women I've ever seen in my life."

Her steps faltered, and he steadied her from almost tripping. "No gentleman has ever said such a thing to me. You are very forward with your words, but I cannot help but wonder if you're saying all the right things to me merely to get your way."

He tapped his nose, grinning. "Ah, well, you shall never know, will you, since you're determined not to tell me who you are. After this night, we're doomed never to meet again." Certainly not if she were a noblewoman who had arrived here by mistake.

"Yes," she sighed, and he wondered if his charm was working on her at all. She was very hard to read, this unorthodox, innocent woman at his side.

"That does not mean we cannot take a little pleasure. Create a small keepsake for us to remember this night by," he suggested, hoping she would fall for his words.

"What do you mean?" she asked him as they stopped before the unlit hearth.

"Well, we could share a kiss. There is nothing scandalous in one kiss, and we're both wearing masks. No one shall ever know who you are, certainly. And maybe, if our paths cross again in a more formal setting, mayhap you'll be tempted to tell me who you are so we may get to know each other better," he lied.

"But you do not want a wife, my lord. You said you only want a mistress, and I shall never fit that employment."

He waggled his brows, and somehow he earned a small grin from her. "Never say never, my virtuous beauty."

"A kiss, you say?" she said after a long pause. "I suppose there is little harm in such a small thing. But I must warn you, even if you kiss very well, nothing else will occur between us, and never will I be your mistress. I have plans, you see. Many of them that I intend to fulfill when I return home, and being your lover is not one of them."

He clapped his hand over his chest. "You wound me. However am I to let you walk away from me after we kiss? I shall be doomed to search for you forever."

She gestured to the many guests, most female, and some who watched them keenly with jealous eyes. "I'm certain that you shall soon find what you're looking for, and you will not need to think of me again."

Corey doubted that very much. Something about the woman drew him, like a moth that wished to fly too close to the flame. He liked her honest, forward manner mixed with innocence.

That she had a friend who was well off enough to employ a maid told him that perhaps she was one of the many debutantes in town. Not that such a thing mattered too much, not at this ball, in any case. But it did make him curious as to who she was.

"I do not want any of the other ladies present. I only want you," he said. "My virtuous beauty."

CHAPTER

FOUR

aphne wasn't sure what had come over her. For a start, she should never be at this ball. A mistake that she would have to explain to Ashley when she returned home. She could only hope her friend was not aware of the error she had made.

But the man before her, tempting and teasing her into being naughty, was an enticement she had not thought ever to face. To be the sole recipient of the handsome man's attention was an elixir to her almost on-the-shelf old soul.

He was handsome, his lips more appealing by the minute. Whatever would she do? Would she let him kiss her as he suggested? What if he tried to force her mask from her face and see who she was? She would be ruined, and then she could never return to Grafton and persuade the vicar to marry her.

"You wish to kiss me, my lord?" she asked again, trying to become accustomed to the word kiss. She had never kissed a man in her life. Not that she had not wanted to. Something told her from her friend's wistful, secret smiles whenever she was around her husband that kissing could be quite enjoyable indeed.

"I do, but only if you wish to kiss me back. We can keep our masks secured and our identities secret if you wish." He took her hand and led her to a part of the room with a free daybed. The transparent curtains pulled aside like an invitation to sin.

"If you agree to kiss me, step inside. I promise not to compel you or ask for more," he said.

This was it. Right now, she needed to decide if she would do as he bade. Would she step into the world of vice for one night only before returning to her quiet country village to live the remainder of her life as a vicar's wife?

Daphne bit her lip, looked about the ballroom, and noted no one was paying them any mind. Each and every one of the guests was occupied with their intended for the evening.

Taking a deep breath, Daphne stepped into the secluded space and went to the daybed. She sat, the many cushions soft and opulent. The little area darkened further when the gentleman unhooked the curtain, closing them inside.

He came toward her, reminding her of a lion stalking his prey. Daphne swallowed, nerves skittering along her skin and making her knees shake. She placed her hands on her legs, stilling them as he sat beside her, his eyes raking her like a physical caress.

She shivered. "I've never kissed a man before," she blurted before reaching for him and kissing him. Except, the kiss did not go as she had planned. Not by half. She slammed her nose against his and their teeth cracked.

"Oh, I'm so sorry." She pulled back and touched her lip,

which already felt large and swollen. "I do not know why I did that," she admitted, heat burning her cheeks. She closed her eyes, thanking God that at least it was dark and hopefully he would not see her mortification.

His hand cupped her chin, and she lifted her face. Cautiously, Daphne opened her eyes and found him watching her, no mockery or annoyance in his eyes.

"You've never kissed a man?" he asked, his thumb sliding over her chin, making her breath hitch. Something about this man compelled her to do naughty, silly things that she should not want to do with anyone who was not her husband.

But never had she seen a man as handsome as this one was, and she so wanted to go against all the rules she had carefully planned for herself the many years living alone and without hope of a husband.

One night of sin. One night of being wicked. What was wrong with that? Nothing in her estimation. And really, was a kiss sinful? It was not like she would go any further than that.

Come morning, she would go back to being the perfect future wife to a vicar just as she was before.

She shook her head, hoping that her fumbling had not pivoted his want of her. "Does that change your thoughts on kissing me, my lord?" she asked him, hoping it did not, but knowing she could do little if it did.

His attention dipped to her lips, and she could see he was thinking about her question. "You're not supposed to be at this ball. Maybe I ought to take you home and spare your blushes?" he said.

Daphne bit her lip, fighting back the disappointment that stabbed at her. She supposed her blundering kiss did not help the matter. Everyone in this ballroom knew how to kiss. Among other things she could not fathom to voice. Of course, he did not want her now.

"I do not believe so, my lord. I think I came here by mistake," she said, wanting to tell the truth, even if that truth resulted in her being escorted from the ball and not experiencing her first kiss. "I believe I was handed an incorrect invitation by a maid. I'm sorry to have wasted your time." Daphne stood, but he clasped her hand, halting her.

"Before you leave, we can still have that first kiss," he offered, the temptation in his eyes making it hard to refuse. What was it about this man that she found difficult to deny?

He stood, towering over her, and clasped her chin. "I still wish to kiss you, even though I should not," he admitted.

Her pulse jumped, and she could do little but stare and revel in his handsomeness that put everyone else she had ever met into the shadows. His voice, smooth and deep, she would keep in her memory, in her mind, and keep it forever when she needed to relive this night.

"You do?" she said, her voice breathless to her own ears.

"God, yes." He covered her mouth with his.

From the moment his lips touched hers, everything changed. Her body thrummed to life and her skin prickled with awareness. She leaned up on her slippered toes, wrapping her arms around his neck, and kissed him back with all that she had.

His tongue teased hers. With her gasp, he made use of her surprise and tangled his tongue with hers. What happened next she would never forget. His mouth took hers in a searing kiss, commanded hers in a way she never thought possible. The sensation tingled her skin and prickled her with awareness. Enjoyable was the optimal word. He was everything delicious in the world, made her body ache and thrum in ways she never had before.

His hands, large and firm on her back, held her against him, and she moaned as the hardened length of his manhood pressed against the top of her mons. Heat pooled between her legs, and she squeezed her thighs together, straining to alleviate the need that thrummed there.

The kiss went on and on. With each stroke of his tongue, the more she fell under his wicked spell. It was too much and yet not enough. She wanted more. She wanted to kiss him forever.

"You undo me," he said, pulling back and meeting her eyes but a moment before he captured her mouth again. One hand slipped into her hair, the other low on her back.

She gasped when his hold slid to cup her bottom. He lifted her until she was equal to his height, holding her on tiptoes. His fingers slid close to her sex, and she moaned, wanting him to touch her there, needing him to soothe the need that rioted within her.

"You're wicked," she professed, wrapping one leg about his hips, undulating her sex against his without reserve or thought as to how she looked to the guests. All she wanted and needed right at this moment was something she could not name.

But she desired it, craved whatever he was teasing her toward like she needed air.

"I want you in my bed," he said, taking her mouth and helping her grind herself against his cock.

Daphne did not know what was happening to her. Her body coiled tight, seeking, needing what he offered. She clung to him and kissed him with all that she had. Copied his every move, every slide of his tongue, the sweet, seductive kisses against her chin. He licked up her neck, biting the lobe of her ear. His warm breath against her ear made her shiver, and she mewled, needing, seeking, grinding harder against him.

"Come for me, my beautiful virtuous stranger," he said, kissing her hard and long.

Daphne kissed him back, her body no longer under her control. It sought, moved, and took what he offered without a care who saw. And then something marvelous happened. Pleasure, unlike anything she had ever known, rushed through her, convulsed, thrummed, and spun out to every part of her body as he worked her against him.

She moaned through their kiss, clinging to him as if he were her lifeline, and at this very moment, she wasn't certain that he was not.

He kissed her for several moments more before easing her back to the earth where she belonged. "I suppose you'll leave me now," he said, his gaze heavy with need.

Daphne took in his form, taking a mental portrait for the remainder of her life. His chest rose and fell rapidly. He ran a hand through his abundant hair, causing it to look disheveled. But it was his jutting, hardened manhood that pressed against his breeches that made heat thrum between her legs.

Would sleeping with the man feel as good as he had just made her? Something told her that would be the case.

She nodded, hating to leave, but knowing she could not stay. If she were to remain, there was no telling what she would do next or what she would offer him. And she could not ruin herself. What she had done was already far past the point of respectable behavior.

"I must go. I'm sorry," she said, reaching up and kissing

him one last ardent time before fleeing into the ballroom, back toward her respectable life and plans to be a vicar's wife.

CHAPTER
FIVE

F or the next several days, Corey lived in a state of
discomfort. His body craved the woman he could
not name, nor did he know if he would ever see
her again.

He stood at the side of the Duke and Duchess of Blackhaven's ballroom floor, playing the embodiment of gentle-
manly behavior and politeness to the fairer sex.

But it was all a show. He was not in London to find a
wife. He needed a lover, and only one would fill that position. It was the sweet little vixen who had come apart in his
arms.

Her first orgasm, he was certain. Even now, a full ten
days after having one of the most sexually fulfilling experi-
ences of his life, he could still hear her sweet sighs. See in
his mind when he closed his eyes the wonder in hers at
what he delivered her.

He secured a whisky from a passing footman and raised
it in salute to his good friend Billington, who stood on the
opposite side of the room.

He narrowed his eyes, taking in the throng of guests,

and wondered how soon he could leave, and if his hosts would notice.

"Renford, good of you to come. I did not think I would get you here," Blackhaven teased, coming to stand beside him and watching his guests with appreciation.

All of this was new to him. Society, the dinners and balls, the promenades, and rides in the park. For so many years, everyone believed he was secluded at his country estate, Grand Oaks. How wrong they were. Fighting for his homeland was where he truly had been, and he could not quite settle himself into this environment as well as he once had.

"Of course I will attend, but for how long is another question. But I'm happy to be invited. How is the duchess? No doubt the preparations of the ball have kept her busy."

Blackhaven chuckled and nodded in the direction of his wife, who stood beside a strawberry-haired beauty. The very one he had seen before Whites on his first day back in London.

"Not at all. The duchess takes all of her duties in stride and does not seem daunted by any of them. And, of course, that she has her friend from Grafton visiting her is much more significant than any ball."

"Is that the young woman standing beside the duchess?" Corey asked. Something about the woman's form seemed familiar, although he could not say what that was. She was a tall meg, had legs that went on for days ...

"Ah, yes, it is. Miss Daphne Raven from Grafton. She's in town securing new gowns," Blackhaven said, clearing his throat.

Corey glanced at the duke and narrowed his eyes at his sheepishness. "Why do I get the impression there is more to Miss Raven than you're telling me?"

"Not at all. She is the most wonderful friend, and I love her as dearly as my wife does. Would you like to meet her?"

Corey shook his head. "No, I'm not up for introductions. I'm not here for a wife, no matter what the gossips about town may say to dispute that fact."

"Very well," Blackhaven conceded, but before Corey could thank his host again for the invitation and slip away unnoticed, he caught sight of the duchess coming their way with the new-to-town Miss Raven.

Corey inwardly sighed, not the least interested in playing the delighted male suitor that this debutante no doubt wanted this Season. Although the closer they came, the more he noticed that Miss Raven was no blushing debutante out of pigtails.

She was a woman, the same age as the duchess, he would guess, and her sparkling green eyes had a knowing, worldly light to them that did not disappoint.

"Renford, may I introduce you to my wife, The Duchess of Blackhaven, and Miss Daphne Raven. Ashley, Miss Raven, this is His Grace, the Duke of Renford."

The tall meg's eyes widened at his name, and she looked up at him before a delightful blush kissed her cheeks. She dipped into an awkward curtsy and mumbled something in return that he could barely hear, nevertheless make out.

The duchess smiled, and he could not help but smile back at the beauty of Her Grace. "A pleasure to meet you, Your Grace, Miss Raven. Our meeting has been long overdue, Your Grace."

"And you," the duchess replied before smiling at her friend and elbowing her a little.

He heard Blackhaven chuckle and knew His Grace had seen his wife's attempt at making her friend speak.

"How long are you in town?" Blackhaven asked him.

Corey shrugged, unable to take his eyes off Miss Raven, although why he could not understand. She was a beauty for certain, not one blemish or scar marring her skin. Her womanly curves all but begged to be caressed, and he had the overwhelming desire to ask about her enjoyment of the ball. Hear her voice.

"Not long. I've come to town to secure some services before returning home. I will not be here the entire Season."

"That is a shame, especially when there are so many prospects for a handsome, eligible bachelor as yourself," the duchess teased, moving to take her husband's arm.

Miss Raven seemed a little lost with her friend not beside her, and she glanced up quickly, meeting his eyes before averting from them just as fast.

She bit her lip, and everything in Corey's body froze. Those lips. Her perfect teeth that bit those kissable lips. Her strawberry-colored hair. Her long legs and breasts that were a good handful, but not more. He had seen her somewhere before, and it was not out the front of Whites.

Dear God, it was her …

His virtuous beauty from Dame Plaisir's masque.

Forgetting where he was, Corey went to take a step toward her and stopped himself. Checked himself, thankfully, before Blackhaven noticed anything untoward.

"Perhaps this evening you are right, Your Grace. I can make an exception for your ball, at least." He held out his hand before Miss Raven and waited for her to look at him.

The moment she did, he was certain, beyond any doubt, that he was correct, and he knew, to his very core, that the woman who stood before him, meek and mild, quiet and subdued, was the very one who had shattered in his arms, rubbed against his cock and came.

She placed her hand in his, and he tightened his hold against her trembling fingers. They did not speak as he led her onto the dance floor before the first notes of a waltz started to play.

Perfect. Just perfect.

He pulled her into his arms and swept her into the dance. After several turns, he finally felt her relax in his hold. "My virtuous beauty. I did not think I would find you again," he said.

Her gaze lifted to meet his, and he chuckled at the fear she all but exuded. He shook his head, tsk-tsking her at her naughtiness. "Are you not going to speak to me? And when we got along so well the last time we were together. I know I have not forgotten you as quickly as you seem to have forgotten me."

She checked about them before meeting his gaze, and for the first time since their scandalous meeting at Dame Plaisir's ball, he saw a little of the fire that drew him as no other had before her.

"I do not know of what you speak, Your Grace," she said.

He laughed, could not help it. The absurdness of her remark was too humorous not to. "My virtuous beauty, I think you do remember and remember well our time together. Shall we take a stroll so I may reacquaint you with how well I know you?"

She rolled her eyes before taking a deep, calming breath. Not that it would help her nerves. She all but trembled in his arms and made him all the more inclined to pull her close, hold her.

Keep her safe ...

He caught himself with the thought and shook such absurd musings free. What was wrong with him? He did not care overly much, for the chit in his arms. Even if he would like to tup her, he wanted no more than that.

Would she even be amenable to becoming his mistress? Was she an heiress? A woman from a family who would never allow such an occupation?

"There is no need for you to remind me of what happened. I merely thought since you are a gentleman, you would not remind me of my atrocious behavior when we met last. But, it would seem your reputation precedes you, and you're incapable of being respectable. Even at an exemplary ball such as this."

He chuckled, enjoying her banter and her annoyance at him. "Where is the fun in not reminding you of how you rode me, Miss Raven?" He leaned forward and brushed her ear with his lips. "I want you to ride me again," he teased. "You made me so rock hard that I ached for days."

She pulled back and glared at him, and he fought to keep a straight face. How delightful this ball had become. How utterly satisfying.

"Well, how very sad and disappointed you shall be, Your Grace. I suppose you had better stop wasting your time with me and go in search of the mistress you're determined to secure, do you not think?"

A laugh bubbled up inside and burst free, and for the first time in a long time, Corey chortled. "Oh, no, Miss Raven. I do not want just anyone. As I stated when we met last time, I want you and no one else, and I shall have you."

CHAPTER
SIX

D aphne did not know what to say or do. Never had a gentleman, and a handsome one at that, been so forward with her before. Not that she could entertain his invitation. To do so would mean ruination for her, and all her hopes of marrying the gentle, sweet vicar would be no more.

Do you really want the vicar when you can have Renford?

He was utterly charming in a naughty, teasing kind of way, and she couldn't help but want to be in his arms again. Since her rendezvous at Dame Plaisir's ball, she had not been the same. Her body had felt all at sixes and sevens after fleeing his side. It remembered what they had done when she dreamed of him, and now, having him before her, his seductive, persuading voice was too much to dismiss.

But she must. She could not be his mistress. Never could she do that to herself or her family. Not to mention all the friends she would lose by choosing that lifestyle.

And what would happen to her when he grew tired of their agreement? She would be retired, possibly with a small stipend, and left to live the rest of her days an outcast.

No, she could not allow such a fall from grace.

"I'm not going to be your whore, Your Grace, no matter how charming you sound while asking me if I will be. I intend to marry, and nothing will stop me from getting what I want. Not even a duke," she stated, wanting him to know she had a life outside their one scandalous evening that she would not give up, no matter how pleasurable that evening was.

"You're betrothed?" he asked, his tone less teasing and sending a cold chill down her spine.

"Well, actually, no, I'm not engaged yet, but I'm in town preparing so that when I return to Grafton and the local vicar asks me to be his wife, we may be married straightaway."

The duke pulled her closer still, spinning them about the room and leaving her dizzy. "Who is this vicar? Is he able to afford to marry?" A deep frown formed between his brows.

Daphne shrugged. "I do not know, but I assume he is financially sound. He is the local vicar and earns a respectable wage, I'm sure."

The duke scoffed and all but rolled his eyes. "The little vixen in my arms last week will never be satisfied as the wife of a vicar. Would you not prefer a more invigorating life to one of prayer?"

"Are you truly asking me that, Your Grace? Do you not think what you're saying is reproachable? I may have very little in my life, possibly the only value other than my reputation is my friends, who are happily and highly situated in the *ton*. I would never throw all that away merely because you want me in your bed. You are very arrogant, are you not?" she stated, watching him, hoping he would stop this madness and speak with a little decorum.

He watched her, and some of his amusement fled. "Very well. I shall not try to persuade you to be my mistress again, but that does not mean I will not attempt to steal another kiss. You did it so well last time."

Daphne growled. Really, the man was impossible. "Tell me, rumor has it that you've been at your country estate these past years. Where is it that you live?" she asked, curious why a man who so desperately wanted a mistress would scurry himself away at a country estate for years on end and not come to London before the 1816 Season.

"My home is in Kent. A large property and one of three that I own. The London house, of course, and a shooting lodge in the Highlands of Scotland."

"I've always wanted to visit Scotland. Is it as beautiful as they represent it in poetry and books?" she asked, imagining the snow-covered peaks and highland cattle that walked them.

"It's harsh and can be deadly. I have a castle, which I repaired extensively some years ago, so it is warm and dry, even if it is ancient. I would like to show it to you one day."

"Unless you're asking me to be your wife, that will never transpire," she said.

"I could invite you and your vicar husband to join my party one year. Mayhap you will be persuaded to join me for a nightcap in my room when everyone is abed."

The idea made heat pool between her legs, and she bit back a curse at how tempting his words could be. "I could never do that, even if I had the worst of husbands. I couldn't break my vows."

He grinned down at her before spinning her to a stop. "I'm certain I could change your mind regarding that. I cannot be the only one here whose body yearns and craves the person in my arms, unlike anything I have ever experienced before. We would do well together, you and I. We would burn like wildfire if we were ignited."

Daphne slipped her hand onto his arm as he led her from the floor. Heat kissed her entire body, and she fought to compose herself. How was she to deny him when he drew her like a piece of string that was tied about her hand, constantly tugging her closer?

They joined the Duke and Duchess of Blackhaven, and Daphne quickly disentangled herself from Renford and stood beside her friend. There was safety when beside Ashley that she did not have when she was around Renford.

"You waltz beautifully, Daph. And you were worried about coming tonight for nothing," Ashley said, smiling at her.

Daphne nodded, trying to avoid looking at Renford, even though she could feel he was watching her, analyzing her, trying to figure out a way to change her mind.

Dear Lord, she could not crumble. While she may allow him to kiss her again, she would never be his lover. That would never do at all.

A ruckus started nearby, two young bucks arguing about horses from what Daphne could make out. As the argument increased, several nearby gentlemen stepped in and pulled the arguing pair away from each other before it escalated into fisticuffs.

Ashley looked at Daphne with widened eyes but did not say a word. About to make light of the situation, she looked at Renford and found him as pale as a ghost and frozen, watching the young pair and nothing else.

On instinct, she reached out, touching his arm, and he started at her contact. "Your Grace, are you well?" she asked him.

He did not look at her, but she could see he was fighting to collect himself. Calm himself, if she were to guess.

"Renford?" Blackhaven also queried when he remained silent.

After what felt like a lifetime, he shook himself free from whatever it was that had started him and smiled at each of them. "If you'll excuse me. I have another engagement this evening," he said, striding away from them all, pushing through the throng of guests as if a bevy of debutantes chased his every step.

Daphne frowned after him, wondering what caused him to turn so odd so quickly.

"Well, that was very strange, was it not?" Ashley stated, looking in the direction the duke had fled.

"Very," Blackhaven said, frowning.

Daphne nodded. "Do you think it was the young men arguing that upset him? Maybe he does not like conflict?" she said, supposing she did not like conflict either. No one wanted to see anyone argue or get upset about trivial matters, even horses. But was that why?

She glanced about the room, looking to see if anyone else was of interest. Maybe he had seen a lady and merely wanted to escape them so he could seek out his next conquest.

"I'm sure he had his reasons," Blackhaven stated, reaching for his wife's hand. "Dance, my love?"

Daphne watched them go, happy that her friend was married and blissful.

"Miss Raven, is it not?" a voice said at her side, the French accent as thick as molasses.

Daphne turned and found a tall, handsome man behind her. She smiled, not wanting to be rude, even though they were not introduced. "I do think we've been introduced," she mentioned. He chuckled at her reminder of etiquette and shrugged.

"When one is as pretty as you are, Miss Raven, why must a gentleman wait to be introduced? Too much time is wasted on such trivial matters, and I would like to dance with you. If you'll do me the honor," he said.

In all truth, Daphne could never understand the rule that a mutual acquaintance must introduce one to be able to converse. She slipped her hand into his and allowed him to lead her onto the floor.

"You're French? Is it safe for you to be here in England so soon after the war?" she asked, hoping it would not offend him.

He chuckled, tsk-tsking her. "Ah, well, perhaps not so safe, but I have unfinished business to tend here in England and will not leave until that is settled. I see no reason why I cannot enjoy my time here while I accomplish all that I must."

"You sound as if your business is very important. What is it that you've to do here?" she asked.

A shadow crossed his face for but a second before he blinked, and it was gone. "I need to settle an account of my family's, and then I shall return to France."

Daphne nodded and threw herself into the dance. "Well, I wish you well with your plans, Monsieur ..."

"Monsieur Henri Caddel," he finished for her. "And thank you. I think they're already coming along splendidly," he said, his smile wide and heartfelt.

CHAPTER SEVEN

Corey woke with a start just as daybreak crept through the window dressings. He sat upright in his bed and placed a hand on his racing heart, certain it was about to jump out of his chest. He threw back the bedding, his shirt uncomfortably damp and clinging to his form. He moved to the side of the bed, ripping it off and throwing it aside. Taking slow, deep breaths, he tried to calm his thoughts. Little good that it did him.

It had been several weeks since he'd had the dream. A nightmare, really, and one that was unfortunately as true as he was sitting there.

The feel of the blade slicing through flesh, the sensation of his weapon scraping bone and finding its mark on his adversary, made him cringe.

He opened his fisted hands and fought to calm down. The war was over. He was back in England, alive and well. There was no reason for him to keep dreaming about the Frenchman he had killed. It was a kill-or-be-killed situation. Anyone would have acted the same.

Are you sure, Renford?

The niggling doubt was always there, taunting him, haunting him, but he would not let it win. He pushed up from the bed and went to where he kept brandy in his room and poured himself a considerable glass.

There was no fire. Still, he slumped into a chair before the hearth and thought about anything but what he dreamed.

The picture of Miss Daphne Raven floated through his mind, and a little of his anxiety dissipated. There was a vixen under that country mouse, and he wanted to taunt it out of her again.

Although, after last evening, she probably thought him a cod's head after leaving the ball as suddenly as he did. He really needed to work on his social responses toward others in volatile situations. He could not, surely not, react as he did perpetually. As much as he tried, his body went out of his control when situations turned argumentative or violent around him. Why he did not know, and try as he might, he could not change his responses.

But also, the moment Daphne had touched him and asked if he were well, he'd never fractured out of his fear so quickly.

He downed his brandy. What did that mean?

Not willing to analyze himself right at this moment or dwell on the past that he could not change, he washed quickly and dressed in buckskin breeches, a new shirt, and a riding jacket before heading for the mews. He would go for a ride, clear his head on the back of his mount and hope that another nightmare did not return this evening.

It did not take his stable hand long to saddle up his horse, and he was soon making his way through the early morning traffic of Mayfair. Several other gentlemen made their way to Hyde Park, but Corey kept his distance, not in the mood for conversation or company.

Reaching the park, he made his way toward Rotten Row and kept his mount at a sedate pace. He reveled in the tranquil setting, the trees that swayed in the slight breeze, the sound of Englishmen talking as they rode, and the sight of pretty ladies who took to horseback at this early hour.

And then he saw her.

He pulled his mount to a stop and studied the lithe form on the back of a large black mare with a long mane and tail. The horse was undoubtedly one of Blackhaven's regal brood, but the rider fit the horse like a kid leather glove.

She looked majestic in her bottle-green riding suit, her strawberry-colored hair that shone when the sun kissed her long locks. They tumbled in a slight curl down her back, and he took a deep breath, wanting to see her hair spread across his pillows in the early morning light.

Waking up to Miss Daphne Raven would be no hardship, and he could not think of anything better.

If only he could have such imaginings. But he could not. They were not for him.

Another gentleman joined her just as Corey went to urge his mount forward, and he pulled his horse to a stop. He'd not seen the man before, certain he did not know him, and yet there was something familiar about his profile, the cut of his jaw and straight nose.

Although surprised at the man's attention, Miss Raven spoke to him amicably enough and moved her mount forward so they may ride together, her groom following close behind.

Corey did not try to interrupt them or push himself in on their little tête-à-tête. He was not so desperate to win

Miss Raven's agreement to be his mistress to do that. Nor did he want the *ton* to think he wanted anything more than that. He did not.

He could not be trusted, not when it came to the safety of others. There was too much he was capable of to allow another to grow close to him, only for him to disappoint them in the long run.

Not to mention what had happened with the last woman he slept with and had fallen asleep beside. A mistake he could not afford to make again.

He closed his eyes, fought not to cast up his accounts at the memory, and turned his mount around. He would return home, bathe and breakfast and spend the day at his club. When around others, at least then, his mind would not dwell on the past. And today, it seemed determined to do precisely that. And he would not let his past break him.

He was the Duke of Renford. A powerful lord of the realm and not some former spy haunted by the many faces of all the men he'd killed, one in particular whom he thought had been his friend. He would not be that.

"**M**iss Raven, what a delightful surprise to find you here this morning," he said, casting a look toward her groom. "You are the perfect picture of a fine English lady out for a ride."

Daphne chuckled at Monsieur Caddel's compliment of her riding attire, which wasn't any different than any other lady here this morning, even though he made it sound as though it were. "I have a good friend who ensured I had riding attire during my stay here. There is nothing special about it. I merely enjoy riding horses," she said, not wanting him or anyone else to think she had come to London to secure a husband. She had one of those in her sight back at Grafton. Not that she was entirely sure Monsieur Caddel was hunting for a wife or merely biding his time with her until someone else caught his fancy.

They turned the horses around as they came to the end of Rotten Row and started back toward the gates she would ride through to return home. She took in the park, beautiful at this time of the morning, and felt the pit of her stomach clench. The Duke of Renford trotted across the row, moving away from her.

She wanted to call out. As to why she could not fathom, and thankfully, she refrained, for when the duke glanced in her direction, he did not acknowledge her at all.

Daphne inwardly sighed. She would much rather be speaking to the duke than Monsieur Caddel. Somehow the duke, even with all his teasing and scandalous innuendo, seemed more genuine than the man at her side.

"Ah, the most sought-after duke in London is here. But he slights you after I have seen him speaking to you at balls and parties. This must hurt you, no?" Monsieur Caddel queried.

Daphne fought not to react to his words. Nor did she want people to think she was after the duke, for she was not. She did not want a husband who would only cause heartache. A vicar was a much safer bet than a rogue duke.

"You are mistaken, Monsieur Caddel. We are acquaintances and not close ones. He can cause no harm to me," she said, not quite believing her own words.

He smiled, catching her gaze. "That is pleasing to know." He paused. "I'm attending the Maddigan's ball this evening, Miss Raven. May I be so bold as to request the first set with you?"

She could not refuse, so she did the pretty and nodded, even though she would much rather not. She did not want to give anyone any ideas of a romantic nature. Except perhaps Renford, but for kisses only. Nothing more.

A terrible declaration she knew. It was devilish of her to want his lips on hers again. But never in her life had she experienced such pleasure and longing than what he had roused within her at Dame Plaisir's ball.

She wanted to feel that intoxicating pleasure again but remain a maid. She could not risk her virtue, not even for the duke. Not to mention he seemed utterly determined to remain a bachelor forever.

"Do you know the duke?" Monsieur Caddel asked, his eyes narrowing on the duke moving farther ahead.

From Monsieur Caddel's queries, she was wondering if the Frenchman wanted to know the duke more than she did. "As I said, we share mutual friends." She met his eyes, wondering why he was so persistent regarding the duke. "He is an acquaintance with the family I'm staying with at present and is close friends with a young lady I knew from childhood." Not that she would explain more than that. She did not know the Frenchman all that well, nor was it anyone's business in truth who she associated with.

"I have seen him before, but I do not know where ... I know that it was before this wonderful Season we're all enjoying here in town." He smiled, still watching the duke with interest. "I'm certain it shall come to me at some juncture, and I will remember. He is not married, no?"

"Ah, no, he is not married or betrothed," she answered, hoping she sounded more aloof with her answer than she felt.

"But perhaps he wants to, no matter what the rumors say to refute this. He takes much interest in you, Miss

Raven. I see I have competition when it comes to earning your trust and friendship."

Heat kissed Daphne's cheeks at Monsieur Caddel's words, and she swallowed several times, trying to force out words wedged in her throat. "There is no understanding between myself and the duke. We have mutual friends, and he was talking to them. Nothing more than that."

"But he danced with you," Monsieur Caddel argued, watching her with a keenness that made unease ripple down her spine.

"You certainly have taken a great inquisitiveness in the duke and me, Monsieur Caddel. Is there a reason we're so interesting to you?" she demanded of him, not liking his questioning. Nor did she need anyone thinking that she wanted the duke when he did not want her. Not for anything innocent in any case, and she had plans to marry. Plans that would mean she did not have to leave Grafton. The village children depended on her and her teachings, and she could not leave them, not even for a duke. Not when becoming his mistress was his only offer.

"I merely like to know who my competition is and their weakness, that is all," he replied, throwing her an impudent grin.

Daphne narrowed her eyes, not entirely certain that was the truth at all.

EIGHT

Accompanied by the Duke and Duchess of Blackhaven, Daphne followed her friends into the Maddigan's ball. The grand ballroom was filled with summer flowers, and the scent of roses, lilies, and wisteria were as delightful as the view. The terrace doors lay open, guests mingling outside as well as in the ballroom itself.

A lovely summer ball that was sure to be enjoyable. Even more so when Daphne spotted the Duke of Renford standing beside Lord Billington. Not that she should think such a thing, but he was handsome, and it was pleasing to be flirted with after years of being ignored.

At their introduction by the Master of Ceremonies, Renford glanced in their direction, but his interest was fleeting before he excused himself from his friend and started for the terrace.

An uncomfortable, annoyed feeling settled in Daphne's stomach, and she wondered at it. Why would she care that he dismissed her so quickly? Maybe his chase of her was as transient as his look had been. That was probably true more than anything else. He was a rake, after all. Looking out only for his self-interests, and she had been candid in telling him she would never be his lover.

That would probably explain why he did not speak to her at the park this morning. She would not relent. Therefore he saw her as a waste of his flirtations.

Daphne shook the disappointment such a realization caused and pasted on a smile as they greeted friends and acquaintances. Monsieur Caddel collected her as promised, and for the first two sets, she danced and played the role of a grateful debutante, but it could not have been further from the truth.

She should return to Grafton. She had her wedding gown measured, and it was being made as she danced at this very moment. She no longer needed to be here. She had seen her closest friend and spent quality time with her. It was time she left and stopped pretending that this life was one that she wanted or liked.

She did not particularly enjoy it at all.

Do not fool yourself, Daph. You've loved the attention from the duke.

She quelled her thoughts and thanked Monsieur Caddel when the dance came to a thankful end. He escorted her back to Ashley before excusing himself.

She let out a relieved breath, not particularly in the mood to answer any more of his buffering questions.

"He's very handsome, Daph. Maybe you ought to look to him instead of the vicar in Grafton. At least he knows you're alive," Ashley said, a teasing grin on her lips.

Daphne smacked her friend's arm with her fan before opening it. "Need I tell you again, my vicar knows that I exist. I teach the children right beside the church every Sunday, and I sometimes help him with his sermons."

Ashley rolled her eyes, her lips thinning into a displeased line. "If he has not seen you and asked for your hand already, then he does not deserve you. I think it would be best if you stayed here in London with me. Find a husband who desires you no matter how devoted you are to God."

Not that Daphne was overly devoted to God at all, but she did enjoy teaching the children and did not want to leave Grafton. Who would teach them letters and numbers if she did not?

"It is only a matter of time before the vicar sees me."

"The Duke of Renford has seen you already, and if I'm any good at seeing when a man desires a woman, which I think I'm fully qualified to have an opinion on, he wants you in his bed."

"He has not even looked at me this evening," she blurted before she could stop herself.

Ashley chuckled at her side. "Aha, you see. I knew there was something afoot. I told Blackhaven, and he did not believe me, but your response is telling indeed."

"There is nothing to convey. He seems to have lost interest," she sighed, seeing no point in hiding her disappointment from her friend. As much as she was determined not to be his mistress, it was lovely being the sole attention of such a handsome man.

"Do you think so?" Ashley said, clearing her throat and nodding in one particular direction.

Daphne looked where her friend noted, and the breath in her lungs seized. Renford, who towered over most in attendance, stood leaning against the terrace threshold, watching her. He appeared somewhat foxed, not to mention disheveled, as if he'd had some secret tryst that had muddled his clothes. His cravat sat half-undone. Certainly, it was loose about his neck and not as precise as it ought to be on a duke.

He looked downright dangerous and utterly, devastatingly alluring.

"I'm sorry, my friend, but that is not a man who has no interest. He wants you, and you need to guard yourself unless you want him too."

Daphne did not know what to say or how to react. She looked about the room and noted others had not seen his interest. A good thing to be sure, for she did not need any gossip going back to Grafton. But then, maybe a little gossip to spur the vicar into proposing would be beneficial.

"Only one way to test your theory, Ashley," she said, flouncing off in the direction of a door on the side of the ballroom. She could feel Renford's gaze like a physical touch, and goosebumps rose on her skin. Still, she did not look at him, merely kept her composure and exited the room without a backward glance. If he wanted her still, he would follow, and then she would decide what to do if she did anything at all except enjoy his attentions before she left London.

There was nothing wrong with a few stolen kisses, after all. She would do no more than that, she promised herself.

No sooner had she closed the door did it open again. A large, warm, determined hand gripped her waist and led her into a room opposite the entrance.

She did not need to ask who was behind her. His feel was as familiar and welcome as she remembered. Not that she was overly happy with him right at this moment. He had been ignoring her all night.

But Daphne had little time to chastise him, for the

moment she turned around, he wrenched her into his arms and kissed her.

Hard.

His mouth worked hers and pulled her into his seductive world. She clung to him, took all that he gave her, and tried not to succumb to his charms yet again.

"The Frenchman is not for you, Daphne," he growled, his lips moving down her neck, teasing the underside of her earlobe and making her shiver.

She could not disagree with his warning, but nor could he think she was his either, for she was not.

You are his already, and you know it.

No. She tried to push him back, but he would not budge. "I'm not the Frenchman's or yours, Your Grace. Even if you try to kiss me and persuade me otherwise," she said.

His wicked grin tempted her to smile back. "Is it working yet? I would so love to have you give yourself to me when you can no longer deny your desire."

"You would not force me so. I do not think even you are capable of that, even if I think you're competent in many things."

"I'm adept at many things. You are correct," he said, his voice grave. "But you are right. I want you to come to me freely."

She shook her head. "You know that is not possible."

"Does not make me not want to try, nonetheless." He kissed her again, walking her backward until her legs hit the side of a settee. Without warning, he lifted her to sit on it, stepping between her legs without shame.

The man was impossible and utterly too sure of himself. Not that she was pushing him away as she should. The wonder of what he would do next was too much to deny, even when she knew she should.

He reached down, and she felt the cool air of the room kiss her ankle and then knee.

She stilled his progress with her hand, meeting his gaze. "What are you doing, Your Grace?" she asked, raising one brow.

"Call me Corey. I do not want to be Renford before you," he said.

Daphne watched him and saw he was in earnest, his eyes all but beseeching her to agree. She nodded, feeling a little at sea from his request. She lifted her hand, letting him have his way.

A hungry expression twisted his handsome features, and when his hand brushed the crux of her legs, had she been standing, she would have crumbled to the floor. His fingers teased her weeping flesh, and she fought not to cry out and bring attention to them.

"You like that, my little virtuous beauty."

"Yes, I like it very much." She should not admit such things to him. The rogue would only make the knowledge work to his advantage, and yet nor could she lie. She did enjoy what he did to her, how he made her feel. The pleasure that had rocked through her before was in reach yet again, and she could not deny herself.

"Ask me to touch you. To stroke you until you come," he ordered, his voice breathless before he retook her lips and stole all thought from her conscience.

"I want you to touch me. Make me feel wonderful," she paused. "Please, Corey," she said, using his given name as he wanted.

Something flickered in his eyes, leaving her wary before he kissed her hard again. His fingers worked her, delved into her, stroked and teased her aching cunny. It was too much, and yet something told Daphne it was also not nearly enough.

She wanted so much more from him, things he would not give.

CHAPTER
NINE

orey was playing with fire. At any moment, a guest wandering the halls could walk in on them, catch them doing unspeakable things, and his requirement of mistress would turn to wife.

But he could not stop. He could not keep himself from touching her, kissing her sweet lips, hearing her breathy sighs when he stroked her wet quim.

She was like an addicting elixir of which he could not seem to rid himself. Since the moment they had met, she had placed some kind of spell on him. He knew she was innocent, and that he should not be doing what he was, but then, she was not stopping him. Not once had she pushed him away, told him no.

If anything, she wanted him to touch her. Could he make her his mistress? Could he persuade her? He wasn't sure he could, but he would try damn well hard.

Her hand fluttered down his chest, tentatively stroking his stomach, feeling her way around his body before her hold dipped lower, and all sensible thought vanished.

Her fingers glided over his cock, stroked him through his silk knee-high breeches, and he groaned. "Touch me, yes," he begged, kissing her hard, pushing his cock into her willing hold.

She grew bold, clasping him, stroking him, and the room spun. He had dreamed of her doing what she now was. He wanted more. He wanted her in his bed. He wanted her as his mistress.

"I will put you up in the most spectacular London town house Mayfair has seen if only you'll agree to be my lover. Be faithful to me," he begged her, groaning when she felt about his balls and stroked him again.

She met his eyes, hers heavy with need. "I cannot do that, Corey. Do not ask me again, please," she begged of him.

Disappointment rushed through him, and he broke away from her, leaving them both unsatisfied. He was being cruel. He knew that, but perhaps if she knew that pleasure only came with an agreement, she would think more about his offer.

She settled her dress about her ankles and stood, righting her composure before pushing past him and walking to the door. "I do not know what your game is, Your Grace. But I do not appreciate being part of it. You know my choice, and while I'm happy to partake in a few stolen kisses, I will not give you my virtue. Not without a proposal of marriage."

"And I cannot give you that," he said, hating that it was true, but it wasn't safe for her or even a mistress to spend a night in his bed. Fucking was one thing. Remaining the entire night in one's arms was another entirely.

It was too dangerous, and he would not risk anyone's life.

54

"A shame," she threw at him over her shoulder before wrenching the door open. He reached to stop her, but it was too late.

The Duchess of Blackhaven with Lady Maddigan stood in the passage talking, their eyes wide with surprise. "Oh, Daphne, there you are. I was looking ..." the duchess's words trailed off when her attention moved past Daphne to him standing in the shadows.

Fuck ...

This could not be happening. His worst nightmare could not be coming to life.

"Your Grace, is that you?" Lady Maddigan asked, narrowing her eyes as if to see him better.

He mentally cringed and wondered if he bolted could they really prove that he was there at all? Especially if Daphne denied all accusations.

But he could not do that. No matter how much he loathed and feared more than anything the marriage state, he could not do that to Miss Raven.

"It is, Lady Maddigan," he said, coming into the passage and wrapping his arm around Miss Raven's waist, who had yet to respond to them being caught alone and in a darkened room. In fact, she seemed to have lost her voice entirely.

"Daph, what is happening?" the duchess asked her friend. Her attention snapped to him once again and shame washed through him. He should have left the chit alone. Had he just found a whore to bed, none of this would be occurring right now.

"All is well, Your Grace. I merely wanted to speak with Miss Raven alone to ask her to be my wife, and she has agreed," he stated, the words like sawdust in his mouth.

He bit back a sigh and pasted a smile on his lips, but he

did not mean an ounce of it. He did not want to marry. Not that marriage to Miss Raven would be so very vile. But the institution itself was not something he agreed with, nor did it suit him. Not after the war, at least.

Not much in the night when he was asleep with his memories did either, for that matter.

D aphne heard the word marriage from the duke's mouth, and yet she could not form a reply. Had they been caught? Why had she not made the duke check the passage before she bolted from the room?

Because he's a cad, and you were angry, that's why.

She could scream at the unfairness of it all. She could not marry him. He wanted a mistress, not a wife, and would no doubt still seek one after their vows. Her life with him would not be in Grafton. He'd stated himself his estate was in Kent.

How many miles from her home was that? Too many to count. No, she inwardly railed. She could not do it.

His hand tightened on her waist, and she met Ashley's and Lady Maddigan's bright and happy faces and knew she could not deny him, no matter how much she wished to. If she did, even her dream of marrying the vicar would be no more. She would be ruined, and any chance of having children would be ripped from her.

"Congratulate us," she said, pasting on the biggest smile she could conjure. "His Grace asked for my hand, and I agreed. I know it's all very sudden, even I do not quite believe it." She glared at him quickly. "But it is true and wonderful, is it not?"

"Oh my darling, I'm so happy for you," Ashley all but

squealed, pulling her out of Renford's hold and into her arms. Lady Maddigan's congratulations followed, and with very little fuss or further comment on them being alone, both ladies seemed pleased by the outcome.

Whether Ashley would feel the same way when she learned of Renford's real reason for stealing her away in the room was another matter entirely. But they were engaged now, and nothing could change that fact unless she cried off from the marriage, which she would never do. She would not ruin herself, not even to please Renford, which undoubtedly it would.

"Is it to be a long engagement?" Lady Maddigan asked. "Or will you treat those in London this Season to a wedding in town? Oh, how lovely it shall be to have a wedding so soon into the Season," she said, clapping her hands together in delight.

Renford cleared his throat, but Daphne could see from the strain about his mouth that he appeared less than pleased by that suggestion. "Of course. We shall be married as soon as it can be arranged. A month is long enough, I'm sure," he said.

"More than enough time," Ashley agreed. "And you shall have your wedding breakfast at our home. I insist as Daphne is under my chaperonage this Season and my closest friend."

Daphne reached out and squeezed Ashley's hand, happy that her friend was so delighted. But what did marriage mean to Renford? He was so opposed to the idea. Did that mean he would be absent more than anything else? Would he spend his days at the club and in the arms of other women? Would he give her children? Would they even have a marriage at all? Or was this just something he would do and leave her to her own devices? The idea left a hollow feeling inside her stomach.

"There is much to discuss, but we should return to the ball." Daphne turned to Lady Maddigan, whose smile was broader than Daphne had ever seen. "Can we please not announce the news this evening? I would like a day or so to process this wonderous news, and the duke and I have much to discuss."

"Of course, Miss Raven. I shall not say a word," her ladyship said, buttoning her lips.

"I shall call on you tomorrow, Miss Raven, Your Grace, and we shall go over the contracts and particulars of the wedding if you're in agreement?" he asked.

"Of course, that will be perfectly fine," Ashley replied.

Daphne started when he picked up her hand and kissed her silk glove. "I shall take my leave, but until tomorrow, Miss Raven," he said before striding down the darkened passage and out of sight.

Ashley came and took her hand, wrapping it about her arm. "Come, we shall go tell Blackhaven if no one else."

They all returned to the ball, Lady Maddigan flouncing off in search of her friends, and something about the glee in the woman's eyes told her that all of London would know of her news before the morning papers were delivered.

They joined Blackhaven, who stood watching the dancers, seemingly lost in thought until he spied his wife.

"Grady, the best of news," Ashley declared, all but bouncing at his side.

"What news is this?" he asked, curious.

"Daphne is engaged to the Duke of Renford. He asked her just a few minutes ago, and she agreed. Is this not the best of news?"

Blackhaven met Daphne's eyes. "Is this true?" he asked her.

Daphne nodded, but she could see Blackhaven was not as pleased as his wife, and she knew the reason why. The same reason she was not enthused. Marrying Renford would mean no happily ever after. If anything, it would be ordinary for him, miserable for her.

CHAPTER
TEN

Corey woke with a start and sat up. He took a deep breath, his lungs hurt at the action, and he clasped his chest, fighting to keep from panicking. He wiped a hand across his mouth, his shirt clinging to him yet again in sweat.

After his spontaneous offer of marriage to Miss Raven but a week before, the nightmares had increased and became more vivid and dark. Danger seemed to lurk in every corner of his mind, taunting him, haunting him that the war wasn't over.

Not for him, in any case.

He threw back the blankets and stared at the wall across from him. Today he was to be married. After speaking to Blackhaven and admitting to almost ruining Daphne, the duke suggested, and Renford had agreed, to marry earlier than planned.

The idea left him cold, and he shivered. A wife living here was not something he had ever wanted to endure. Not so much for himself, but for her.

Marriage to him would be no life at all. If anything,

Daphne would soon come to hate him for what he had forced upon her.

Corey rang for his valet and ordered a bath. He went through the motions of getting ready for the day. One that, should he have wanted a wife, ought to be of joy and expectation.

It was not. He could not rouse one tidbit of excitement.

His valet entered, and he was soon in a bath, the warm, fragrant water going some way toward calming his nerves. He shook his head, laying back against the tub. There would need to be rules and limitations placed on Daphne since she was to spend her first night here.

The most important and one that would never be able to be broken was that she could not spend a night in his bed. Their sleeping arrangements needed to remain separate and defined. If only to keep her safe.

The clock ticked away the hours he had left as a bachelor, and it was all too soon when a footman notified him that the carriage was waiting outside his house.

"Will there be anything else you require, Your Grace?" Thomas asked, opening his bedroom door.

"Please ensure that the duchess's room is prepared and ensure the lock is in working order. I do not want any trouble, Thomas," he said, pinning his valet with a hard stare. One that his servant knew not to disobey, especially since his valet knew what occurred when he was asleep.

"Of course, Your Grace. Everything will be as you asked upon your return." He paused. "From myself and your staff, may we wish you very happy, Your Grace."

Corey nodded, accepting the felicitations with grace. It was not his servant's fault that he carried a wound from the war that would not dissipate. No matter how much he tried to forget, at night, when he was asleep, his memories were always there to remind him.

The carriage to church took very little time. As agreed upon with Daphne, the marriage was only for close friends and no family, as neither he nor Daphne had anyone left to attend their weddings. A select few, and since he was friends with very few people, he was surprised to see several affluent and influential families on Daphne's side of the aisle. Billington was, of course, on his, but otherwise, everyone who was anyone in the *ton* was on the other.

He walked up to the vicar and greeted him, steeling himself to get this ceremony over with so the day could end, and he could be alone.

This was not what he wanted, and he could not pretend otherwise.

Daphne let Ashley fuss over her at the church doors before Blackhaven held out his arm for her to take. "Are you ready, Daph?" he asked her, his smile warm.

"As ready as I hope to be," she said, kissing Ashley before her friend disappeared into the church to find her seat.

A pianist started to play, and Blackhaven escorted her into the church and up the long aisle. Daphne could not stop her smile, no matter how much she tried to keep her composure. All her childhood friends, the Woodvilles, the Yorks, and now their husbands, sat waiting for her, supporting her on one of the most important days of her life.

She looked ahead, and the nerves that had plagued her for the past week returned twofold. The Duke of Renford watched her, but she could see he wasn't looking at her.

Not really. If anything, he seemed to be looking past her, trying to ignore that his future bride was coming toward him.

She had hoped that seeing her in her blue silk gown with a pretty lace bodice would spark some interest in him, but from the moment they had been caught at the Maddigan's ball, he'd been distant. Sometimes she had even wondered if he liked her at all.

But they had been caught, and there was little either of them could do but make the best of a bad situation.

The thought of becoming his wife, a duchess, and all that would entail was no small position. She hoped she would make him proud, and maybe he would not be so distant in time.

They came to the top of the aisle, and Blackhaven bussed her cheeks before giving her hand to Renford.

Daphne tried to meet his eyes, but he would not look at her. The vicar was more interesting, apparently, than looking at his wife-to-be. She fought not to protest, to rail at him for being so cold. This was no more her fault than it was his. He had followed her into that passageway in the first place. She had not asked him to. And as for that matter, she certainly did not ask for him to push into a vacant room and do such wicked things to her that others may observe.

Throughout the ceremony, Renford stubbornly refused to look at her, even when he placed one of the most beautiful diamond-and-sapphire rings on her finger that she had ever beheld.

She felt her mouth gape and snapped it closed before anyone noticed. Never had she possessed something so beautiful, that was hers from this day forward. The thought of being a duchess was so foreign that she might as well pretend to speak Spanish.

"I now pronounce you husband and wife," the vicar stated, smiling at them both.

Daphne forced a smile on her face as they turned to their guests. Renford thankfully kept hold of her hand as he led her down the aisle, Ashley and several of her friends kissing her cheek as they passed.

The wedding breakfast was to take place at the Duke and Duchess of Blackhaven's London home, and they were soon in the Renford carriage heading back to Mayfair.

"Are you going to talk to me at all today, Renford?" she demanded once they were safely away from any of their friends who did not need to hear them quarreling merely minutes after they had said their vows.

"What is there to say? We're married, you're a duchess, and I'm still a duke. There is little more to discuss," he said, his voice lifeless and bored.

She narrowed her eyes at him, unsure how this whole predicament had become her fault. "You cannot be angry at me for what happened today. You followed me into the passageway. I did not ask you to."

"I also did not ask you to storm out of that room and straight into the path of Lady Maddigan and your friend. What were you thinking? Unless that was your plan all along to ensure you gained a duchess's coronet."

Daphne took a deep breath, trying to calm her temper, but it was no use. She would not be blamed, no more than him, nor would she be termed a schemer.

"You're just upset because I would not be your mistress, no matter how sinfully delightful our time was when we were locked away alone. I had plans, too, Renford. Plans that did not involve you, London, Kent, or wherever it is that you have your country estate. If anyone has reason to be angry, it is I, not you. You will no doubt still continue to live your life the way you always have. In time, possibly within weeks of this day, I shall hear some gossip involving you and your new mistress just as you wanted. So please do not play victim to me. I've lost more today than anyone. You, as a man, will live as you please. I shall have to play at being a duchess."

"Oh, yes, of course, because that is such a displeasing and offensive title to carry. Do tell me again, what was it you wanted to do instead?"

His question ignited a fire in her that would not be doused. "I intended to marry the vicar in Grafton as you know, and continue to teach the village children letters and numbers."

He stared at her for several seconds before bursting out laughing. Daphne fisted her hand, wanting to punch him square in the nose.

"You, marry a stale, virgin vicar and be a governess to village children. Do be serious, Daphne. You cannot think I ever believed you wanted that over being a duchess."

His sarcasm against innocent children made a pain thump hard in her chest, and she glared at the prig. "You bastard," she yelled, losing some of her decorum. "How dare you mock what I did for those innocent children, many of whom, without my teaching, would not be able to better their lives. Make a future that is brighter than the one their parents lived. Do you have no empathy at all? You are a duke. You have tenants and servants, all of whom no doubt have children. Are you such a snob that you cannot see past your own self-greatness?" she asked, unable to think otherwise.

"You cannot tell me that marriage to me did not cross your mind the moment I showed interest."

She scoffed, sure it had not. Had it? "You think too highly of yourself."

"Let me be clear, Miss Raven," he said, using her old name. "We shall discuss this evening after we return home how our marriage will work, and you will obey me, or there will be hell to pay."

She crossed her arms over her chest, doubting that very much. She would not obey him or anyone. At nine and twenty, she was too old to start taking orders now. "Obey you, Your Grace?"

"As per our vows," he reminded her.

She sneered, moving to look out the window. She could not study his aggravating face a moment more. "Those vows are outdated, just like your declarations regarding our marriage. Do not be so sure I'll do anything you say."

CHAPTER
ELEVEN

Corey smiled and laughed and made happy during the wedding breakfast, but he could not forget the argument that he had had with Daphne just moments after their nuptials.

He watched her across the lawns of the Duke and Duchess of Blackhaven's London home and could see that she, too, was playing the make-believe game of happily ever after, and all of the people milling about them seemed to believe it.

His stomach knotted. Each time she thought no one was watching her, the mask of an elated bride slipped, and despair filled her pretty green eyes. The realization that maybe she had made a mistake in marrying him.

Well, they had both made one of those, and there was little they could do about it. But he could keep her safe. She would not be permitted into his room, certainly not when he was asleep. He could not trust himself. Too many times, he'd woken in odd places in his room, holding different objects as if he were defending himself in his dreams and reenacting them when he was not awake.

A dangerous situation, even for his staff. But to add a wife to his troublesome living situation was not ideal. He did not want to hurt her. He did like Daphne very much, and he certainly desired her. She sparked a need in him that no one ever had. He closed his eyes, wishing he had made a different choice at the Maddigan's ball.

If only he had not followed her. If only he had held her back before letting her leave that room!

"Your pretend visage is slipping, Renford. You had better amend it before anyone other than myself makes note of it," Billington said, handing him a whisky.

Renford downed it, needing it more than he imagined. "Am I being obvious? I should watch myself more. I do not want to make this day worse for my bride than I already have."

"And have you?" Billington asked, watching him keenly.

Renford ran a hand through his hair, guilt churning his gut. "Yes, I've already ruined her first moments with me. But she knew I did not want marriage, for several reasons I'm not willing to discuss, but that does not change the fact that ..."

"You were caught alone together?" Billington finished. "Blackhaven told me, in confidence mind. I shall not say a word to anyone. The duchess told him, but I think he guessed already when Miss Raven and the duchess returned to the ballroom that something had occurred to bring about a proposal so soon."

"I did not want to marry her or anyone. But I cannot change our lives now. I merely must make the most of what we have."

"Miss Raven is a beautiful woman. Surely marriage to her will not be so hard. Not to mention she grew up with the Woodville girls, all of whom have married titled men, including myself. She will often be out and socializing, going to balls and parties. It will only be when you travel to Kent that you shall be truly alone."

The thought made him shudder. He could not be alone with anyone after what occurred in France. No, it was too dangerous.

Mayhap it would be best if she stayed in town indefinitely and he only traveled back during the Season ...

"There is much to think about, but I'm certain we shall come to a mutually agreeable agenda," he said. "I received an invitation to a ball yesterday from a Monsieur Caddel. Have you heard of him? Is he new to town?" Renford asked, wanting to change the subject.

"I do not know him well, but Lord Davies has brought him several times to Whites. I have spoken to him there, and he seems amicable enough, but French, of course, which is a challenging thing to be so soon after the war. His family is old aristocracy, and they somehow kept what they had in France during the revolution and have not suffered from that fight."

"Hmm," Renford mumbled, uncertain himself why the Frenchman was in London. Was it not odd that he was here? A man whose country only this time last year they were at war with?

"You remained at Grand Oaks the last few years. What kept you from town? We often wondered," Billington said in a teasing tone.

"My father did not leave the estate in the best of health," he lied. "It took some time to make it profitable again and to repair the estate and tenant houses. Not to mention the church and estate grounds. There was much to do," he fibbed, still unable to fathom how easily it was for him to quip something so false, and to a friend. His years as a spy in France, mostly due to his father's connections with the Duke of York were convenient, of course, but still, he did not like lying to one of his closest friends. Should Billington ever find out who he was and where he had been the last few years, he would be shocked, hurt, possibly, that he had not told him. But then, Renford was sure he would understand too. The safety of England and its people was often hanging by his ability to lie, to meld into the crowd, to become someone he was not. Any Englishman with an ounce of loyalty to their country would understand his reasonings.

"Well, it is good to have you back, and I'm certain the late duke would be very proud of you for all the work you've put into your birthright," Billington said.

"Thank you," Renford replied, looking back to his wife and knowing that particular problem would be less easy to face and live with for the rest of his life.

Daphne ignored her new husband as much as she could. Outwardly she was all smiles and laughter before her friends. Talking of wedding nights and the days ahead as the new Duchess of Renford. But inside, she was seething with annoyance. The blood in her veins still bubbled after their argument in the carriage.

How dare he make her one day, her wedding day, that she was unlikely to repeat again, into a yelling match across the squabs of a carriage.

Did the man have no values at all? Was he so disappointed in their union that he would tell her that there would be rules that she would need to adhere to for their marriage to work?

What kind of man said such a thing to a woman on the day they married?

She sipped her champagne, possibly quicker than she ought, for the opulent grounds swam a little in her vision, but it was beyond reprehensible.

That he dared blame her for all of the strife they now found themselves in was not something she would ingest. If anything, he and his rakish wiles were the reason they married, and when he declared his rules later this evening, she would let him know what he could do with them.

A supporting hand came up from behind, and she started at the feel of her husband.

"Are you a little foxed, Duchess?" he asked, meeting her eye.

The laughter she noted in his tone made a little of her annoyance dissipate, but she would not let him distract her with his good looks or false care. Butterflies in her stomach or not, she was mad at him, and she would not let him forget it.

"Well, if I am," she whispered, not wanting anyone to know they had argued merely hours before. "It is your fault. If one cannot enjoy the minutes after one's wedding, one should at least enjoy one's wedding breakfast."

He lifted his glass of whisky and tapped it against hers. "Very well, cheers to that," he said, downing his drink.

She watched as his tongue ran along his bottom lip, and thoughts of his mouth on hers bombarded her mind. She frowned and glanced at the lawn, needing to gather her thoughts. She was angry with him. Heavens above, she could not desire him at the same time.

Could she?

Maybe drinking so many glasses of champagne was not such a good idea after all.

"You are looking a little pink under the morning sun. Perhaps too much celebrating?" he said with a pointed glance at her glass.

The man was as infuriating as he was seductive. Even so, his teasing was much preferable to them arguing like two old fishwives.

"Not enough, I would suggest," she said. "And anyway, I'm an old married woman now. I may do whatever I like."

"Within reason," he quipped.

She looked at him, needing a further explanation of his statement. "What do you mean by that? Care to elaborate?"

He shrugged, smiling and nodding in welcome to a guest who wished them well. "While at home, our marriage may not be the norm, but then maybe it will be. Who knows with society marriages, but when we're out in public like we are now, we shall appear a unified front. No one needs to know how it was that brought about our nuptials. That is our business and no one else's. By playing the doting roles of husband and wife, it will allow our children to be more favorable as matches. No one wants to marry into a family where the duke and duchess are at war."

"So we're to have children?" Excitement thrummed through her blood at his mention of them having children. It had not been a subject brought up in the week before they were married. In fact, she scarcely saw Renford leading up to today. He had kept his distance and only called on her once, other than the times he played the doting fiancé at balls and parties.

"I should think you would want children. Do not all women?" he stated, matter-of-fact.

She shrugged, sure some women would prefer not to, as their right, but she did want children. Desperately so, and the sooner, the better. "While I cannot answer for others of my sex, yes, I do wish for children. I am nine and twenty."

He choked on his whisky and met her eyes, his glassy with tears. "You're nine and twenty?" he blurted.

She glanced about, hoping no one heard his exclamation. "Yes, is there a difficulty with my age?" she asked, staring him down and daring him to say there was.

Thankfully for his own self-preservation, he did not.

TWELVE

Corey cleared his throat. The whisky, having gone down the wrong orifice, made his eyes water and his throat burn. He did not mean to react the way he had to Daphne's age, but she did not look nine and twenty. Of course, he knew she was older than most debutantes. He just had not known it was by ten years.

"I meant no offense. In fact, I'm glad you're closer to my age than not. You're more formidable as a woman, which I had glimpses of the first time we met."

She raised her brow, and he doubted he had ever seen a woman look less pleased in his life. "And what do you mean by that?" she all but spat.

"Only that," he said, choosing his words carefully. "When you started to enjoy yourself, you forgot all the rules and proper etiquette drilled into us since birth and merely allowed feeling and enjoyment to take precedence. In other words," he said, leaning close, so near that he could smell the scent of jasmine. "You came alive, Daphne."

He watched her swallow and fight to remain unaffected

by his closeness. Being this near to her again brought back all the memories of that night.

He desired his wife. He had wanted Daphne in his bed for some time, and now there was no impediment to why he could not bed her.

They could enjoy each other quite a lot, so long as she obeyed his rules and remained locked away and safe in her room. Safe from the nightmares and questionable actions he did in the dead of night.

"And I suppose you're such the rogue that you're going to tell me that you are the only man in England who can bring me to life. Since up until we met, I must have been dead or dreary at the very least."

He grinned, unable to deny enjoying her quick wit. She was all fire and brimstone, his new wife. "Perhaps we could slip away indoors for a moment's peace and see if what I say is true. Test that theory that I can make you come alive in my arms."

Her lips pursed, and he could see she was thinking about his words. For several minutes she studied the guests and did not speak before she nodded. "Very well, Your Grace. I do need a little respite indoors. Would you escort me, please?" she asked him, placing her hand on his arm.

He covered her hand with his and started them in the direction of the terrace. "You have a room in the house, care to show me where it is?" he asked.

A rosy hue kissed her cheeks, but she nodded. The house was large, almost the same size as his own, and had a similar layout. Daphne led him through the ballroom, into the foyer, and up the main staircase, passing several footmen and maids as they went.

She turned right on the first floor and opened a door halfway down the passage. "This is my room," she said.

"Well, it was my room. My trunks were taken down earlier today, and only a few things are left here for the wedding breakfast."

Corey moved into the space and glanced about. The furnishings were of high quality, and the bedding luxurious, as he expected for a ducal property.

He turned and faced his wife, pulling at his cravat to loosen it. "Close and lock the door, Daphne," he ordered her.

He bit back a grin, seeing that she did not like to take orders, but after a slight pause, she did as he told her, the snick of the lock echoing about the room like a promise of things to come.

Nothing was stopping them now from enjoying each other. He'd wanted her in his bed from the moment he'd first seen her, and now he would have the opportunity.

He wrenched off his coat and waistcoat, laying them over a nearby chair before pulling his shirt over his head.

She stood at the door, her bottom lip lodged between her teeth, watching him, her eyes wide with wonder. He supposed she probably hadn't seen a man naked before.

Without thinking further about it, he kicked off his shoes and wrenched his breeches off as well, throwing them aside. The sight of her watching him, enthralled by his nakedness, made his cock hard, and he wrapped his hand around his engorged dick and stroked himself. He wanted her to see him, to watch and learn what he liked.

"You're still clothed," he murmured, picturing her gaping, delicious mouth about his cock, sucking him, bringing him to climax down her throat. "No need to undress. I can fuck you just fine in that gown."

Without another word, he strode over to her, scooped her up in his arms, and carried her toward the bed. She let out a little squeal of surprise before letting him do what he wanted. Wanting her to feel him, every part of him, he slid her down his front, letting his cock press against her body.

She bit her lip, color high on her cheeks. Never had she appeared so beautiful.

Corey shuffled on the bed, lying on his back, watching her. "Get on, Daphne. Come and enjoy the ride."

When she did not move, he reached for her. She crawled over him, sitting on his lap. He helped her settle her dress out of the way and let her become accustomed to his cock, which pressed against her sex.

"What am I to do now?" she asked, her hands tentatively pressing against his chest. He swallowed, fighting for control. He didn't want to scare his new bride from the bed chamber, but nor did he want to wait. His body ached for release, and he wanted to claim her, make her his and no one else's.

"Lift up, and I'll guide myself into you," he said.

She nodded and did as he bade, but the moment he pressed his cock to her core, she froze.

"I do not know if I can do this. I'm scared it'll hurt, Corey," she said.

The use of his given name undid the rake that raged within him, and he flipped them onto the bed, settling between her legs. "We'll take it slow, Daph. Do not worry."

He reached between them, stroking her, working her sex until she was wet and undulating against his hand. She was so responsive, so willing and eager.

His balls grew tight, and he knew it was time.

"I'm going to make love to you now," he said, unsure where this attempt to be meek with his new wife came from. Even so, he would not stop, he did not want her to be pained by their first time, not that it would not be uncomfortable, but he certainly wanted to do it again and did not want to scare her away.

"You will feel full and strange, but I hope not to hurt you," he explained.

She nodded, biting her lip, and he bent his head and kissed her, doing all he could to calm her nerves.

D aphne lost herself in the kiss with Renford. His mouth worked her with slow, deep strokes that warmed her in the most delicious places.

She was not so naïve that she did not realize that her first time with a man would be uncomfortable, but the taste of him, his warmth and body pressing against hers, made her want to give herself to him.

Made her want him.

She slipped her legs about his hips, and he growled at her surrender. "That's it, darling, open for me," he breathed. "Let me in."

He pressed against her wet core and did not relent. Her body opened, blossomed for his manhood, and with the barest of stings, they were one.

He kissed her neck, his breathing tickled her ear, and she shivered, wrapping her arms over his shoulders, reveling in the feel of his strong back. For so long, she had wanted him just as they now were. He had made her feel so wonderful the two times they had been alone, without consummation, that she had hoped that being intimate would lead to more pleasure.

So far, she was not disappointed.

Slowly he started to move, rock into her, and the sensation, although strange and unfamiliar, teased an inner part of her that longed to be touched.

"I like this," she admitted to him. He met her eyes, his darkened with a hunger she had not seen before. He kissed her, hard and long, their tongues tangled, their breaths mixed, before he thrust into her with a force she had not expected.

Daphne sighed, the sensation strong and delightful. "Again," she asked, unable to believe she was being so brazen.

"I'm more than happy to oblige," he said, thrusting into her with long, steady strokes that stoked the fire within her to a roaring flame.

She could not get enough. She wanted more of him, all of him. Yet he continued to rock into her as if there were no rush, as if they had all the time in the world.

They did not. They were supposed to be outside, enjoying their wedding breakfast with their friends.

"You're mine now." His words were hoarse and brooked no argument.

She nodded, knowing that was as true as their marriage this day. She was his, as he was hers, and how she loved that fact. Their future started now. He may wish to impose rules and marriage regulations, but nothing was set in stone. There was always room for negotiation. And indeed, when she was in his arms as they now were, he was in her power as much as she was in his.

And that gave her more authority than he may think, or ever knew he was sharing.

CHAPTER
THIRTEEN

Corey had never felt such an overwhelming feeling as the one that scored through his blood right now. Never had he wanted to do more than please the woman beneath him. He wanted to hear her scream his name, to participate, and want him as much as he wanted her.

The thought was both troubling and thrilling. She was his now. His wife, his to make love to whenever he could persuade her to allow him into her room.

He would want to do so often.

She lifted her legs higher on his hips, and he gave her what she wanted. He thrust into her, pushed and teased her toward the pinnacle they both sought.

Her sweet body clutched his, her cunny tight and milking him toward climax.

"You feel so good, Daphne," he groaned, his balls tight, his cock weeping for release.

She bit her lip and rocked against him, and he felt the first shudder of her orgasm as it ripped through her, dragging him along with her.

He came hard and fast, pumped his seed deep into her pitcher, and let her ride his prick to the end of her pleasure.

Her eyes glazed with wonder and satisfaction, and he felt that sentiment through every part of his being. He aimed to please her, and he was glad she was delighted.

"Well," she breathed, her words labored from their exertion. "I did not know it would feel as good as that. I think marriage may suit me very well." She grinned at him in such a naughty manner that his cock twitched at the idea of doing it all over again.

But this was her first time with a man, and he did not want to make her sore. Not when he wanted her again tonight. He slumped beside her and made himself comfortable in the bedding. She rolled into him, partly lying on his chest. He could see her eyes closed, a small, wistful smile on her lips.

For the briefest moment, he reveled in their cocoon of satiated bliss before fear curdled in his gut. He sat up, disengaging Daphne, and climbed off the bed.

It took him only seconds to gather his clothing and dress. Out of his peripheral vision, Daphne sat up and watched him, her face one of puzzlement.

"Is something the matter?" she asked. "Can we not lay together for a time? We're married now. No one can say anything about us stealing away." Sweetly, she tapped the bed beside her, and as much as he wished he could lie next to her, have her fall asleep in his arms, he could not.

The idea of him waking up, her small, delightful neck being squeezed by his hands, sent ice through his blood.

"One of my rules is that we're not to fall asleep together, Daphne. I'm a duke, and you're now a duchess, and we must both get plentiful rest," he lied, trying to buffer the hurt and rejection she would feel at his words. "I will call on you in your room whenever you wish for company, but more than that, please do not ask of me, for I cannot give it," he said, hoping she would not ask nor argue the point. His mind was made up, and there would be no changing it. He did not want to hurt her, and if this was the only way he could ensure he did not, he would sacrifice that part of marriage so many couples took for granted.

"You do not wish to sleep with me? You only wish to copulate with me and nothing more?" she questioned.

Her query made his terms sound seedy and cold, and he supposed they were, but he could not tell her she had married a man who was haunted by the past. No one knew of his history, and to protect himself and his family, which now included Daphne, it had to stay that way. Nor could he tell her she had married a madman who, at times, could not control himself.

"That is what I wish. But I promise what we do will be anything but copulating. That word does not emulate what we just accomplished," he said, grinning and trying to make light of the situation.

A small frown formed between her brows and he could see she was trying to understand. But she would not. He had not told her enough for her to understand, and for that, he was sorry, but it was the way it had to be.

A spy never divulged they were a spy. To do so placed Daphne at risk, even if the war was six months over.

"Then I am sad for us," she said, slipping from the bed and righting her dress. His heart skipped a beat at how pretty she looked today. His wife ...

It would take a lifetime to get used to that term.

A little while later, Daphne stood beside Ashley at her wedding breakfast and watched as Renford, her husband, laughed and charmed several guests across the lawn.

"And where did you disappear to, Your Grace?" Ashley teased, laughter in her eyes. "Several guests were wondering."

Daphne smiled, but she could not find the situation funny. Nor could she fathom what had occurred. "Apparently, there are rules in our marriage that I'm to obey," she blurted. "We're to make love, but neither of us can sleep in each other's rooms." She met her friend's eyes and frowned. "Do you not think that is strange? I know for certain you sleep in Blackhaven's suite of rooms."

Ashley cleared her throat and glanced in the direction of Renford. "Did he say that to you?" she asked.

"He did, and was adamant that we're not to. I do not understand why, however," she said.

"I do not know either. I wish I did, for it may give you some insight, but I cannot." Her friend paused in thought for a moment. "Maybe he just needs time, Daph. You're only new to the marriage, and it'll take some adjustment to get used to being married and living with each other. I know it was strange for me when I first married Blackhaven," she explained.

Daphne supposed that might be true. It was odd that she was now a married woman, a duchess for that matter. Men, as well as women, would take time to adapt. In time, when he became used to her sharing the same house, the same dining room and library, and every other part of the house that was now as much hers as it was his, he would relent. He could not keep her at arm's length forever. It would not be possible, surely?

"I'm sure you're right. I will give him the space he's asked for at rest and hope that as the weeks go by, he will concede on that rule," she said.

The orchestra that sat under a copse of trees started to play a waltz, and she smiled as Renford made his way over to her for a dance.

He bowed toward her, and several ladies sighed at the gentlemanly and romantic gesture. Daphne took his hand and let him lead her onto the terrace, not as sure as others that he was being romantic at all but merely playing the role of a newly married man.

He did not want her in his bed after all. How unromantic was that?

He swept her into his arms as the dance commenced, and she soon fell under his charming spell. His ability as a gentleman, his charming smile, and his grace on the terrace dance floor was unmatched, and yet, beneath all that proficiency, something was off, wrong, about everything.

What husbands did not share a bed with their wives?

"Is something the matter, Daphne?" he asked, watching her keenly.

She shrugged, not sure it was wise to bring up the subject again. "I was thinking, Your Grace. You do not wish to sleep in my suite of rooms, but can I join you in yours? Or am I prohibited from your room?" she asked, genuinely curious as to what other rules she was to obey.

"You do not need to come to my rooms. I shall call on you." He threw her a smile that did not reach his eyes before staring at something over her shoulder, not meeting her eyes. "My room is the same as yours in any case. It is nothing exceptional or anything you're missing, if that is your concern."

"And if I do call on you, will you send me away?"

"I shall merely walk you back to your room, and we shall be alone there," he explained.

"And if you fall asleep in my bed, what will happen? I'm starting to think you believe I shall gobble you up in the middle of the night and you'll no longer exist."

He laughed, but Daphne found little amusing. Never had she heard anything so absurd in her life, and nor could she understand. There had to be a reason. He could not favor sleep so much that he would toss her out of his bed as soon as he found release. What kind of unfeeling, rogue of a man did that?

The wickedest duke in London …

She inwardly cursed the thought and thrust it aside. He may have had a bad reputation before their marriage and had wanted a mistress …

Was that why he did not want her to sleep in his bed? For if she did rest there, then he would not be able to sneak away and find pleasure with the woman he no doubt wanted more than a wife.

If she slept in his suite of rooms, his nighttime antics of carousing all over London would be something he could not hide from her. Despair tinged the hope she had that their marriage, which had started off wrong, may be righted in time. Their marriage, like so many others in London, would be in name only. At least if she had married her vicar, that marriage too might have been a loveless match, but at least she would have had the village children and schooling.

Here in London, she had nothing.

CHAPTER
FOURTEEN

L ater that evening, Corey lay back in a bath in his suite of rooms. He was married now. The thought was not as vile a thought as it once had been, but nor did it sit well with him either.

Knowing that a woman, his wife and duchess, now lived under the same roof as he was a little disconcerting.

But more so than that, the need to keep her in her rooms at all times during the night was paramount.

He could hear the muffled murmurings of her speaking to her maids as she settled into her room. He could imagine her inspecting her private space. Did she find it comfortable and appropriate? He hoped she did, for all his dislike of marriage and having a wife, now that he did have one, he did not want to disappoint her or make her life unbearable.

So long as she continued to adhere to his rules, they would get along famously well.

The door to his room swung open, and he turned in the tub. His wife entered as if the chamber were hers to rule. "Please leave, Thomas," she said, gifting his servant a sweet, please-adhere-to-my-request smile. His valet did as he was asked and left without a reply, closing the door quietly behind him.

"You're not supposed to be in here, Daphne," he drawled, reaching for the soap. "We spoke about this."

She came and knelt beside the tub, taking the soap out of his hands and working it between her fingers. It lathered, and his cock twitched, thinking of other things her nimble fingers could be stroking.

"It's not bedtime yet, so there is no harm in me being in your room. And in any case, it's our wedding night. I can only presume you have plans for us this evening?" she said, one eyebrow suspiciously raised as if to say *you better have something planned*.

He had nothing planned other than bedding her. He frowned. Did she expect an opulent dinner downstairs followed by a nightcap and seduction by firelight?

In the heatwave London had been experiencing, a fire was not on his high-priority list, nor was romance.

Instead of answering her question, he took her hand and pulled it beneath the water, wrapping it around his cock.

She bit her lip in the way that drove him to distraction, but it was what she did next that spun his world off its axis. She wrapped her fingers around his engorged manhood and stroked him with exquisite skill.

He sucked in a startled breath, having thought she would require more tutelage than he had already given her, but that wasn't the case. She was already better than she believed herself to be.

"Strip off your gown. I want to see you. All of you," he commanded. The idea of seeing her naked the utmost important thing in his life. He had not seen her thus but knew to his very core that she would be magnificent.

Without question or trepidation, she reached for the buttons on her gown. An annoyed frown marred her forehead, and she turned around. "Help me with the fastenings. They're being difficult," she ordered, meeting his eyes over her shoulder.

Corey did not need to be asked twice. He reached for her, making quick work of the fastenings before she did the rest with little trouble.

She faced him, untied her corset, throwing it aside before reaching for the hem of her shift and stripping it from her body. She stood before him in nothing but her silk stockings, tied by thick, pink ribbons about her slender thighs.

He swallowed.

Hard.

His cock pressed against his stomach, and his balls ached for release.

Do not hunger for your wife, or you'll be under her power.

Corey ground his teeth. He would not succumb to his wife's charms, even if she harbored more than he had first thought. He licked his lips, wanting to take her hardened nipples into his mouth and suckle them, bite and kiss them better.

God damn. What he wanted to do to the woman was not worth mentioning.

"Get in," he ordered her, his voice deep and hoarse, unrecognizable even to him. "Leave the stockings on." He cleared his throat as she stepped into the water, seemingly knowing where she should place herself without being asked.

She straddled his legs, her cunny pressing against his cock. She sighed, rolling her hips against him, using him to tease her aching flesh, and he reached for her, held her hips still, lest he lose what little control he had of his gentle-manly decorum.

Not that he ever had much to begin with. He wasn't known to be a gentle lover. Just a man who fucked well and took his lover along for the ride, no matter how long or short that was. But things were different now, even if he had not wanted them to be.

"Eager, wife?" he asked her.

A knowing smile tipped her lips, and he could not wait another moment. He clasped the back of her neck and wrenched her close. For a moment, he held her but a hair's length from his lips, watching as her eyes darkened in hunger, her breasts rising with heightened need.

Their eyes met, held, and not for his life could he look away. An odd weight settled in his chest as he closed the wee space between them and kissed her.

She was like a flower opening up under the morning sun. She kissed him with a skill that left him breathless, his body aching for release. For a woman who had not kissed or been with a man intimately in nine and twenty years, it had not taken her long to learn the talents that would tumble him to his knees, should he be standing.

Their tongues tangled, their lips dominant and taking what they craved. Never had a kiss enthralled him as much as this one did. It stole his breath and his wits, and not for the life of him could he stop.

He wanted her.

All of her.

Now.

He lifted her and thrust into her wet notch. She threw back her head, her long strawberry locks falling over her shoulders and back. Her breasts rocked with every thrust, and his mouth grew dry at the vision she made.

Never had he seen anyone as perfect or beautiful in the act of lovemaking.

Fucking, he corrected his thoughts. This was not love-making. They were both taking what they wanted. Grinding and working their bodies to a frenzy.

Toward release.

"You're so beautiful," he confessed, leaning against the tub and watching her with pleasure.

Her fingers clawed into his shoulders as she watched him too. "So are you."

D aphne did not know what had come over her, but she knew she had to play this seduction game just as well as Corey if she were to keep her husband occupied in her bed more than anyone else.

She could not stand the idea of him bedding another woman. Certainly not now that he was hers.

And he was. All hers, and she would not give him up without a fight.

She shifted upon him, enjoying the friction they created where their bodies joined. Being with him in water was new and exciting, not to mention soothing a little of the pain at being new to all of this coupling they were taking part in.

The sweet sensation of expectation teased her where they merged, and she knew he was pushing her, taking her to where she would have that brilliant end that he always delivered.

She craved to feel blissful again. To feel him deep within her as she shattered about his manhood.

Daphne rocked against him, moaned when he took her deeper, harder than before, and she shattered. Pleasure rocked through her, carrying her to a remarkable place he could only take her to.

She heard herself cry out his name as his cock hardened and thickened within her, and heat spilled into her aching core. She rode him, pulled him along for this marvelous ride, and did not stop until the very last of her tremors subsided.

Her breath labored, she collapsed against his chest, his heartbeat loud and fast against her ear.

"Who knew baths could be so wonderful? I certainly did not know."

He did not answer, but his hand slid delightfully against her back in circular motions in a soothing, calming manner.

She sat up and slipped off him, moving to the other end of the bath, and watched him for several moments, merely drinking in the handsomeness of her husband.

Husband? What an odd name and one she had not thought to use. Not with the man before her, in any case. But he was by no means hard to look at, and she knew he caught the attention of many, not just her.

But how to keep it and not find out he had gained his mistress as he wished? How to make him trust her enough to allow her into his heart and bedroom for more than just a quick tup?

"I suppose you're going to ask me to leave now?" she said.

A muscle worked in his jaw before he nodded. "It is best, Daphne. You will have to trust me that I know what I'm talking about."

She felt the soap brush her leg, and she picked it up, cleaning herself quickly. "Very well, I shall do as you ask, but I hope this is not a long jeopardy situation to which I must adhere. I do not think it is healthy for a husband a wife not to share a bed."

He shrugged, and his nonchalance toward her opinion hurt.

She stood before him and let him take his fill of her before she left his quarters. "Are you certain you do not wish for me to stay?" she asked brazenly.

His mouth gaped, and a little bit of her pride returned. He was not so unaffected by her. In fact, she could use his attraction to her advantage if she was prudent.

He cleared his throat, rubbing a hand across his jaw. "It is for the best. Goodnight, wife," he said.

"Goodnight, husband." She stepped out of the tub and wrapped a towel around her body. She walked from the room, not bothering to dress any further.

This was her home now, after all, and she was the duchess. She could do whatever she liked, including walking from her husband's room, barely clothed. He had to see what he was missing, after all.

FIFTEEN

Corey attended the next evening's ball with renewed contentment. After last night's escapades with Daphne, he was certain she had come to accept, if not agree with, his rules regarding their sleeping arrangements.

After his bath last evening, he had left his house and headed to Whites, where a game of speculation had been in play. He soon joined in, content to while away the night in the company of friends.

At some time during the morning hours, when the sun kissed London good morning, he had stumbled through the doors, several hundred pounds lighter of blunt, but at least sleep would come easier. Uninterrupted rest from both his wife and the nightmares that plagued him so often.

He smiled at the sight of Daphne dancing with Lord Astoridge, a good friend and one he could trust. But the moment the dance came to an end, his ease dissipated.

The Frenchman, Monsieur Caddel, sauntered up to her, smiling in the confident French way he had about him. He undoubtedly sought to feed her as many compliments as he could think of.

His wife did not seem to mind if her bright eyes and wide smile were any indication. A knot settled in the pit of his gut, and he downed his whisky, watching and wondering if he ought to introduce himself. They were married now, after all. Maybe the Frenchman had yet to hear the news everyone else in London had.

But before he could do as he had decided, the Frenchman picked up his wife's hand and led her onto the dance floor. He pulled Daphne into his arms as a waltz started to play.

The blaggard would not dare take the one dance he had been waiting for and claim it for himself. Corey's attention dipped to where the man's hand settled on Daphne's waist.

Were his hands where they ought to have been? Or a little too low on her back?

A wave of anger he had not experienced before simmered under his blood, and he took a deep breath, letting it out slowly. His wife would be loyal to him, as was her duty. She would not make him a cuckold mere days after their wedding. There was nothing wrong with an innocent dance between two people already acquainted. It was not as if they were slipping off onto the terrace together.

Alone ...

He narrowed his eyes and caught sight of Billington, who joined him. "Renford, how is married life treating you? You and the duchess must attend a dinner I'm hosting a week from tomorrow. Invitations were sent, but we've yet to hear from you," he said.

"I have been occupied elsewhere," Renford stated, continuing to watch his wife.

Billington chuckled, a knowing light in his eyes. "You're newly married. My darling wife and I thought that you may be occupied with other things in the evening and too busy to attend a tiresome dinner."

"We would be happy to attend," he said, possibly a little too keen and quick even for his ears. "That's if my wife does not want to attend another ball and dance more waltzes with Monsieur Caddel."

Billington choked on his wine and glanced toward the dance floor. "Come now, it is but a dance. She married you, did she not? I do not think she's looking to further acquaint herself with anyone," he said.

Corey knew he sounded like a jealous ass. A position in life that was both new to him, and an annoyance. To be jealous meant weakness, and he was never that. Had he ever portrayed those emotions in his life, he would not be here right now enjoying the ball.

He scoffed. Who was he kidding? He loathed London and the Season and all that it entailed, and there was no use pretending otherwise.

"Let us hope that she is not, for I will not be made a fool."

Billington studied him a moment before he sighed. "Come, a good conversation is happening on the terrace about Napoleon and his antics after he was captured and shipped to Saint Helena."

Corey took one last look at his wife, still gliding about the ballroom floor, and followed Billington. The cool night air went some way in bringing down his annoyance at seeing Daphne in the arms of another man. Not that such a sight would usually grind on his nerves, but they had not been wed long. She could have waited a month before being particular with anyone else.

Mayhap he ought to still look for a mistress if his wife would be so friendly with other men.

"Renford!" the Duke of Romney said, clapping him on the back in greeting. "We were just talking about Napoleon. How the night he was captured, he turned as pale as a ghost, they say."

"And his buckskin breeches as brown as shit," Billington interjected, laughing.

Corey smiled and nodded in agreement, but none of that was true. The Frenchman had put up a good fight, and there had been no cowering or shitting of pants. He had been a worthy opponent, and Corey knew better than anyone the truth of that night, for he had been there.

Unfortunate as that truth was.

D aphne did not know where Renford had disappeared to but never mind. Monsieur Caddel, her dance companion, was thankfully happy for her union with the duke and seemed most pleased that she had married.

"Congratulations again, Your Grace. I'm certain you will make the most delightful duchess London has ever seen," he stated, not an ounce of teasing in his tone.

"Have you met my husband, Monsieur? I think it is time I introduced you to him."

He pursed his lips and thought about her question for a moment. "I know of him, of course, by reputation, but I do not know him as well as you, Your Grace. I know the duke has many strains on his time, and I do not wish to add to them. But it is men such as myself and others I'm sure who will look upon the Season and see that its luster has lost a little of its shine with you married."

She chuckled at his flattery. She supposed he wasn't so

bad as she had started to believe. "Thank you again, Monsieur. But I'm certain the duke would be more than pleased to meet you. I should think being a Frenchman in England right now isn't the easiest journey, but I'm pleased you're here, and I hope you're enjoying yourself."

He nodded and glided her to a stop when the music ended. He escorted her to the side of the room and procured them both a glass of ratafia. "The war is over, and all of us must move forward from that time. I know that my business here in England will soon end, and I shall have to return home and marry myself."

"That is lovely," Daphne said, pleased that he was not looking at her to fill any emptiness in his life. She had never been good with admirers, having never had any in the past. Not that she could say Monsieur Caddel was an admirer, but he was certainly seeking her out more than any other lady. "Is there a young lady already waiting for you back home in France?" she asked.

A small, wistful smile touched his lips before he nodded. "There is a young woman. A little scandalous perhaps, as she was a favorite to my brother, whom I'm sad to report I lost during the war."

On instinct, Daphne reached out and clasped his arm. "I'm so sorry for your loss, Monsieur Caddel. That must be hard for you and your family to endure."

"It is very hard indeed, you are right. But my time here in London will undoubtedly cure me of any lingering melancholy. It is what my brother would wish for me to do."

"Of course," she replied. "And you mentioned the lady. A favorite of your brother. Does that mean she's also a favorite of yours?" she asked him.

"She is the best of women, and I hope to win her heart.

My brother was the eldest, you see, and his sweetheart deserves the title I now hold as much as anyone. She did not deserve to lose her love the way she did, and I did not deserve to lose my brother. I will make it as right as I can for us all."

Daphne nodded, but something about how Monsieur Caddel declared his intentions gave her pause. There was something odd about his manner when he spoke of his brother; a coldness entered his eyes as if whatever he intended to do to heal his family's pain may cause misery elsewhere.

He glanced down where her hand still clasped his arm, and she pulled away, dread settling in her stomach when she noticed Renford's cold gaze watching her from across the room.

"I hope you're able to heal in time, Monsieur Caddel," she said, swallowing the nerves that settled in her stomach at the sight of her husband striding toward them with determined steps that could only be termed as deadly.

Was he angry at her? Did he think she was too familiar with Monsieur Caddel? She meant no harm in being kind to a grieving man, even if he were French.

"Darling," the deep, chilling baritone of her husband said as he joined them. He pinned Monsieur Caddel with a look that would send lesser men fleeing from the room.

"Your Grace," Monsieur Caddel said, bowing in greeting. "Your wife is wonderful company. You ought to keep her closer. Otherwise, I think you shall find her much occupied this Season and not at your side."

Daphne glanced at Monsieur Caddel, wishing he had not said such a thing, for it was not true. Was the man baiting her husband? She looked back to Renford and found him glaring at the Frenchman, and if looks could kill, Monsieur Caddel would also be as cold-stone dead as his brother.

Not what anyone wanted to see in the middle of a *tonnish* ball.

CHAPTER
SIXTEEN

"Indeed," Corey drawled, wondering what the little Frenchman was up to warning him in such a way. He was not a man to cross and could break the little fellow's narrow neck with merely a stretch and twist of his hands. He watched Monsieur Caddel knowingly smile at his wife, and Corey bit down hard on a retort.

He may not be able to kill anyone at a ball, but he could certainly ruffle him up when no one was looking. "I shall have to keep that in mind, will I not?" Renford took hold of Daphne's hand, placing it on his arm. "If you'll excuse us," he said, not giving a reason before he pulled his wife away.

Daphne came with him without protest, and he glanced at her, noting that she seemed unfazed by Monsieur Caddel or his own mood. "Monsieur Caddel seems to find your company particularly stimulating," he said, hoping he kept the annoyance that such a fact had on him out of his tone. "I'm starting to think he was a favorite of yours before our scandalous interactions made marriage to anyone else impossible."

She chuckled and sighed as if she found his conversation annoying and troublesome. "Of course not. I hardly know Monsieur Caddel. I think his coming to speak to me and making conversation stems from wanting company. He is French, after all, and there are few fellow Frenchmen in England right now. He is possibly lonely."

"And rightfully so. Were we not at war with France?" he spat, the memories of those days as clear and taunting as ever.

"We are no longer. I know there was much trouble and a lot of death between our two countries, but we must move forward. Napoleon is on Saint Helena and will not leave again."

"He escaped Elba. There is no saying he will not try again."

"He will not," Daphne said with more conviction than he had on the matter.

They strolled on the outer fringes of the ballroom floor, and oddly enough, he had no desire to settle her with any of her friends and leave her to her own devices. While he may not have wanted a wife, that did not mean he had not found their conversation of late to be most welcome.

Talking to Daphne meant that his mind did not wander to the past and dwell there. She was a comfort he did not know he needed.

"I should think you lost many friends in the war. Is that why you're so cold toward Monsieur Caddel?" she asked him.

Corey nodded, wishing he could tell her the truth of his role in the war against France, but he could not. That was a secret he would take to the grave.

"Many childhood friends, both titled and commonfolk alike. My childhood friend, who became the head gamesman on my estate, was killed at Waterloo. My head stable hand's son also perished. He was but seventeen years old. Too young to die."

Daphne's other hand came up and clasped his arm, pulling him close. "I'm so sorry, Renford. Maybe when we return to Grand Oaks after the Season, we may be able to do something for the families in mourning. Erect a memorial or dedicate a part of the village to their allegiance to England. Their sacrifice."

He pulled Daphne to a stop, the idea lovely and heart-felt. Why had he not thought to do such a thing? It would give the families of his village a place to go and mourn and give thanks. "I think that is a splendid idea, and I will think further on the matter. See what I can organize with my steward before we return to Kent."

Her wide smile and bright eyes at his compliment of her idea caught him unawares. She was so stunning and thoughtful. He could see why she had so many lifelong friends who would do anything for her. The Duchess of Blackhaven was foremost in his mind. How Daphne had remained on the shelf for so long still confused him. Men were blind, it would seem.

"I'm so pleased you think so. I know there is much healing required in England. This is but one small step toward reaching that end."

If there was ever an end to grief and memories of war. Corey did not think there was. "Shall we dance?" he asked her as the first notes of a minuet started to play.

"Yes, thank you," she said, her face alight with joy.

Not that he wanted to give her any hope that their life when at home would change, but that did not mean they couldn't enjoy each other's company while out at balls and parties. There was no harm in dancing or talking, such as they were. They were married, after all, and would be for a very long time.

They slipped into their places among the other dancers just as the dance commenced. It was a lively tune and required faster steps than other dances. Daphne's laughter as they moved around the room, weaving and changing partners before coming back to each other again, made him smile.

"You're a good dancer," she said as they moved together in the next figure. "Has anyone told you that, Your Grace?" It was a complex dance, but one he had mastered at the age of ten.

"I enjoy dancing more than people may think. In fact, I enjoy most activities. I am not a dull fellow all the time, Daph," he said, hoping to make her smile and move their conversation away from the talk of war and the horrors that incurred.

It did not work.

Her brows drew together, and she appeared confused. "Do you really mean that? You're always so subdued and serious. The only time I have not seen you so was at Dame Plaisir's ball. And I should not have been there in the first place."

Corey inwardly swore, not wanting her to think that. Not always. Certainly, there were times when he was severe and aloof, but he did not want to be like that to her. He wanted her to feel as though she could come to him always. Just not at night when he was asleep in his bed.

"I'm not serious all the time. I just do not wish to be caught up in the gossip and scandals of the Season. I find it most wearisome after being away for several years. My social manners are not what they used to be. But that does not extend to you. Please remember that."

"Oh. I see." She frowned but seemed to accept his response.

He was different from every other man she had ever met. A man who had secrets and needed to keep it that way, lest they hurt her. Life was unfair, and he carried a burden that would not dissipate, no matter how much he wished it to.

"Do you always tell everyone what you are thinking?" he asked, hoping to distract her from his faults.

"If they're seeking my council and require insight, I do. I cannot see the point of having an opinion and keeping it to myself. That is not healthy," she said. Was she lecturing him?

He swallowed, knowing how true her words were. He had not been healthy of mind for some months, and he knew it stemmed from his time abroad. What he had done and what he suffered to survive. "I promise to be the best husband I can be to you, Daphne. I hope you know I do not mean to come across as harsh. Nor do I want the rules in place at home to be seen as a cruel slight. They are not. I do them because I care for you, and as hard as it is to understand, to keep you safe."

She did not reply. He wished he could tell her what he was thinking and feeling. Unburden himself, but he could not. To do so would only burden her, and that was not fair at all.

"Can you not tell me your deepest fear?" she asked him. "I feel as though you're hiding something from me. Something that I could help with if you only let me do so."

Corey could not believe her insight. How did she know he had so many dark and angry secrets boiling away in his mind? Memories that haunted him in the dead of night taunted and terrorized him.

"I'm a duke, my dear. I have no fears," he lied just as the dance came to an end.

She curtseyed and stepped back, giving him space. Corey wanted to haul her back into his arms and seek her council, unburden himself, but steadfastly he remained mute.

"I have no fears," he repeated, hoping that sounded convincing to her.

One of her eyebrows rose, and she did not look persuaded at all. "Very well. I shall accept your answer. Will you accept mine?"

"Of course," he stated, disliking the space between them.

"I will not force you to love me, Renford. I simply wish to be friends. Lovers. I wish to make our marriage enjoyable for us both. I wish for you not to regret our union," she told him, her eyes on his. He could see the fear in her green eyes, and he swallowed, hoping he did not fail her.

"I do not regret marrying you. Not at all, and I want all those things too. Truly I do."

"Well then, I am pleased that you do not regret marrying me, but I am sorry that you do not wish to know me, or tell me your deepest fears. I would like the opportunity to know you better, but I suppose if you will not relent, there is little I can do," she said and curtseyed again before leaving him alone on the dance floor.

Guilt plagued him, and he followed her, but at a more sedate pace. He would like to get to know her better, but that would be where such conversations had to end. Daphne did not deserve to experience his nightmares as he must.

CHAPTER
SEVENTEEN

Daphne woke with a start at the horrendous cry that echoed throughout the house. She sat up and listened for several minutes, waiting for her heart to return to its regular beating before she realized where the sound was coming from.

Renford's room.

She waited for several moments, and all remained quiet before she heard it again, a muffled, tortured moan that made the hair on the back of her neck stand on end.

She threw back the bedding and started for Renford's chamber, not bothering with her dressing gown. The closer she came, the more tormented the cries grew.

"Renford?" she called, knocking on his door. She tried the handle, surprised it was unlocked, and peeked into the room. The curtains were open, allowing moonlight to stream into the space and she could see her husband thrashing on the bed, the bedding kicked to and fro in his unconscious battle.

She entered and closed the door, tentatively moving closer to his bed. "Renford?" she called again. "Corey?" She placed a hand over his brow, stroking his face, and felt the sheen of sweat kissing his skin.

What was happening in his dream that would cause such a reaction? His bedding appeared as if he had battled some unknown assailant.

"Corey?" she called again, and before she knew if her words had awoken him, he wrenched her onto the bed, pinning her beneath him, a cold, hard blade pressed upon her neck.

Daphne shoved against his shoulders and cried out when the knife pressed deeper. "Corey, stop!" she managed. "Corey, it's me. Daphne." She clasped his face and tried to shake him to his senses. What on earth was he dreaming of? "Corey!" she screamed, and this time, the pressure against her neck dissipated. Corey blinked, and his brown eyes focused on hers before horror filled them.

"Daphne," he said on an exhale, his breathing labored. His attention snapped to the knife against her neck, and revulsion crossed his features.

"Dear God, I'm sorry." He threw the blade, its metal clanging against the bedroom floor.

She pressed his hair away from his face, trying to soothe him as much as she tried to regain her wits. What had just happened? And why was Renford sleeping with a blade? Dear God, he could have killed her. Tears filled her eyes as relief swamped her and she fought not to break down.

"Are you well?" she asked him in a trembling voice.

He slumped to the side of the bed and stared at the ceiling, his hand rubbing his brow as if it pained him. "Jesus, Daphne, what are you doing in here?" he asked, his voice hoarse.

She reached up to feel her neck, glad to note there wasn't any blood trickling from where he pressed the blade

TAMARA GILL

against her skin. What on earth had come over him to do such a thing? Was his nightmare so horrible that he thought she was his imaginary assailant?

"I heard you cry out, and when I came into the room, you were thrashing about on the bed. I merely thought to wake you up," she said, looking at him.

He met her eye, and she could see pain radiating from his. "When you hear me, you must not come in again. Not under any circumstances," he said.

Daphne did not like the sound of his command or what it implied. It made little sense to leave someone who was having a nightmare to continue to dream within it. "If you did not sleep with a knife, my coming in here would not have been so very dangerous."

He cringed at her words and rolled her onto her back, pinning her to the bed with his weight. "We agreed that you would not sleep in here," he said, reaching for the hem of her shift and pulling it upward. "When you're alone with me, it gives me ideas," he said. He closed the space between them and brushed his lips against hers, the softest touch that left her wits reeling.

"Stop trying to distract me, Corey." She wiggled beneath him, which only helped him do away with her shift altogether.

"I do not know what you mean, Your Grace," he said.

His hand pressed against her mons before his nimble fingers stroked her aching, needly flesh. She needed him. Wanted him, even after the scare she just had.

He kneeled between her legs and did away with the nightshirt he wore. Daphne felt her mouth gape as his body was revealed. He was glorious, chiseled so much so that even the most perfect male physique would be green with envy. Without thought, she sat up a little, reaching out to touch the muscles on his stomach.

His breathing hitched at her touch, and she bit her lip, heat pooling between her thighs. "I want you," she admitted, lying back down.

He came over her and thrust into her welcoming body with a force that left her reeling. She clutched him and held him tight as he pumped relentlessly into her.

"Daphne." His mouth was savage and demanding upon hers.

She kissed him back with all the ability she possessed, wanting him to give her what she craved, what they both wanted.

Pleasure.

Her body thrummed, tingled with the promise of what was to come, and she did not have to wait long. He reached between them and rolled a sweet little spot on her quim.

She moaned. "Yes, Corey. Just like that," she begged him, and then she felt the first tremors of her orgasm as it ripped through her, fast and robust.

"Daphne," he moaned as he strained, pumping his seed deep within her.

He slumped to her side, his arm lazily over her stomach for several minutes as they regained their breaths.

Daphne reached for the bedding, pulling it over them both before settling at his side.

"Do not do that, please," he said, his voice muffled by his pillow.

She looked at him and found him watching her. "Surely you do not want me to leave now? Not after what we just did," she said, gesturing between them. Disbelief mixed with pain tore through her, and she could not believe what he was ordering her to do.

"It is best that you return to your room. As you can see from before, I'm a restless sleeper. I will only make you tired," he explained, but she did not believe him.

He did not want her in his bed. He did not want his wife in his bed and never had.

She threw back the bedding, and as naked as the day she was born, she walked from the room, heedless of anyone who saw.

Corey cursed himself to hell at his treatment of Daphne. She did not deserve such harshness, especially after taking her to his bed to distract her, them both really, from what he'd done.

How perfect could life be if his wife could lie beside him after sex? For him not to fear the unknown or what he was capable of. But this evening had been yet another reminder of the danger he posed to others, and he would not hurt her.

He would not hurt anyone else ever again if he could help it.

Except maybe the Frenchman if he kept singling out his wife ...

He watched her saunter out of his room without an ounce of clothing on and marveled at her pride. She was determined to ignore him, he would give her that credit, but it would be best not to.

He had hurt before. He could do so easily again and not know he had done it until it was too late.

The door to her room slammed shut, and he sighed. She would be so much better off had she not married him. Had he not been the unrepentant rake that he was and followed her into that room that night, none of this would have happened.

So many if onlys that he would drive himself insane if he kept thinking about them.

He could not stay here. He needed to leave to gain some fresh air and perspective on what he would do with his wife and her demands on him.

Without second-guessing himself, he jumped from the bed and dressed quickly in the attire he'd worn to this evening's ball. He would head to his club or Blackhaven's gambling den. Anywhere he could so long as it would dispel what his mind conjured at every waking moment.

The image of his wife on his bed, pliant and willing to do anything he wished. So long as he allowed her to stay warm in his bed.

He strode from his room and heard the door to Daphne's room open. "Renford," she barked. "Where are you going?" she called after him.

"Out. I need air," he said, glancing at her as he turned onto the stairs. The hurt that crumpled her features tore at his soul, and he forced himself to take the steps, to move toward the front door and the freedom that it promised.

He did not wait for the footman to open it or order his carriage from the mews. He merely strode past his servant and wrenched it open himself.

The fresh air hit his face, and he took a deep breath, forcing the cooling air deep into his lungs. A hackney turned the corner, and he strode into the street, hailing it. "East End," he commanded, climbing into the carriage and slumping against the squabs.

He would go lose several hundred pounds at the gambling den, drink liquor and lose himself for several hours. At least when he drank to excess, he was less likely to dream.

Daphne will not understand ...

No, she would not, but what could she expect? He had not wanted a wife, and he had been honest about that fact long before they were caught alone. This was the type of marriage many noble ladies endured, and Daphne would soon get used to the same. She could not expect more. He could not change.

The war had changed him enough, and he would never be the same again.

EIGHTEEN

The following morning Daphne could not look at her husband as he sat at the head of the breakfast room table and remained oblivious to what he had done. Or perhaps he did know after his late-night departure and did not care how she felt about it.

She jabbed at her eggs, shoving them into her mouth with little decorum as she thought of all the ways she could hurt him with the cutlery in her hand.

Even now, her eyes felt heavy and stung from the many tears she had shed. How could he have dismissed her so last evening? Sent her away from his room, but moments after they had been intimate. And not only that but then leave the house altogether to go to nobody knew where.

"You are quiet this morning, Daphne. Is everything well with you?" he asked.

She scoffed and let her fork clatter to the table. "Are you truly asking me that? After how you treated me last night? I have never felt more like a doxy in my life. But perhaps that is what you want? You certainly scuttled out of the house soon enough after I left your room. That makes me think you were barely satisfied."

Renford's visage flickered from one emotion to another before he looked to the two footmen serving them. "Leave us, thank you," he ordered. "Close the door on your way out," he barked as an afterthought.

He stared at her for several moments, and Daphne refused to look away. She could stare at him just as well as he could stare at her, and after last evening, she would not listen to or enable any of his excuses. No one could excuse themselves from treating their wife so disgracefully.

"I do beg your pardon, madam," he said, his tone lacking emotion. "I never did such a thing."

She shook her head, wondering if he had lost his memory in the few hours he had been away from home. "After being intimate, you kicked me out of your room while I was still trying to catch my breath," she spat. "Were your adventures outdoors so very mind-numbing that you forgot what you did? Or how you think the request made me feel?" She wanted him to acknowledge that he had been cruel, unfeeling, and cold.

Why, she did not know, but she wanted to. She did not want their marriage to continue in this way. Go from speaking as equals one moment to being cold and aloof the next. "You have nightmares. I understand that. But surely, if I were to be with you, to wake you the moment you start them, it would be better for you. By sending me away, I fail to see how that is helpful."

"It is helpful for me, as it enables me to sleep well, knowing I cannot harm you or anyone. Look what happened last night. I could have sliced your throat without even knowing I had. Right now, you could be dead. Is that what you want?"

"Of course, that is not what I want," she argued. "But you heard me. I think you ought to stop sleeping with a weapon and sleep with me instead. Not be alone anymore."

Not that she knew why he had such dreams, but what would it hurt to change how a person lived, to try to see if that modification alleviated the problem? "I think you're using your nightmares to keep me from you. I know you did not want marriage, but we are married, and I do not like that I'm sent away like a dirty little secret you're trying to keep from our staff."

He stared at his breakfast, and she could see the muscle in his jaw working as he took in and thought about what she said. Was she making any sense to him? That she did not know, but she hoped she was.

"I did not want to marry you any more than you did me, but we are husband and wife now. I cannot feel like I'm doing something wrong should I fall asleep in your arms."

"I do not want you to feel that way, Daphne. I only want you to remain safe."

"What has happened that I'm not safe in my husband's arms, Corey? Please tell me so I can understand," she begged of him.

He ran a hand through his hair and sighed. "I cannot tell you that, and please do not ask me again. It is not a debatable subject."

"Not a debatable subject? Whyever not?" She pushed her chair back and slapped her napkin on the table before striding toward the door. "I'm going out," she said, not bothering to wish him a good day or explain where she was going before wrenching the door open.

When she did not hear his footsteps coming after her, she asked a maid to fetch her bonnet and gloves. Within minutes she strode from the house and made her way along

Mount Street. She would walk to the nearby Berkeley square and cool her heels. Try to calm her temper.

Renford was so frustrating, and she was unsure what to do or say to make him trust her. Barely a week into their marriage and they were already arguing. However would they survive the remainder of their lives?

"Your Grace?"

She turned and inwardly swore at the sight of Monsieur Caddel walking purposefully toward her, his top hat and walking cane clapping loudly on the cobbled path.

"Monsieur Caddel," she said in welcome, while in truth, she wanted to tell him to bugger off and leave her alone. The last thing she felt like doing right at this moment was being polite to the opposite sex and making small talk. She had no interest in speaking to anyone of the opposite sex. "How good to see you."

His broad smile looked too wide for her liking, and not for the life of her could she force one on her face.

"It is excellent indeed. I did not know you lived nearby," he said, glancing about as if to spot the location of her home.

"We live on Mount Street," she said. "That is the Renford's ducal residence just over there," she said, pointing. "Has been for hundreds of years, or so I have been told."

"How is the duke this morning, Your Grace?"

The pit of Daphne's stomach clenched, and as much as she did not want to speak the next words, she knew she must. "He is very well, Monsieur Caddel. Was there a reason you asked?"

"Hmm, well, I do not think it is my place to say, Your Grace." He stared ahead, frowning, and she knew whatever he wanted to tell her would not be to her liking.

"Would you like to walk with me?" she asked him, not wanting to be rude, but needing to walk. Whenever she had a problem she could not solve when back in Grafton, a good, brisk walk always helped, and she did not want to stop and chat. But walk and chat she could do.

"Why, thank you, Your Grace. That would be most welcome." They walked for a minute or so in silence, and Daphne refused to ask further about what her husband had been seen doing that would make Monsieur Caddel state such a thing about Renford. If he had any intention of telling her, he would soon enough.

"I think a walk is just what I need, Your Grace. I must admit that I was out until the very small hours of this morning. London has many diversions, does it not?" he stated.

"Very much so," she agreed. "However, I was to bed at a reasonable hour. Last night's ball had been very crowded."

"Yes, yes it was." He paused. "I did see the duke out later, however. He did not seem the least tired when I saw him at Blackhaven's gambling den. Quite the opposite, in fact."

The temper that Daphne had been fighting to simmer started to boil once more, and she took a deep, calming breath. Renford would not dare make a fool of her on top of ordering her out of his room like a hired bedmate. But then, after his obstinance this morning, there was little she did not think he could do, especially when he was trying to avoid blame.

"The duke has many pulls on his time."

"Indeed." Monsieur Caddel chuckled. "It is early days in your marriage, Your Grace. I'm sure such escapades are but teething problems that you will soon muddle through."

Daphne stopped on the sidewalk and met Monsieur

Caddel's eyes. "I do apologize for what I'm about to say, Monsieur. But I'm not a person who likes to muddle my way through life and try to find the truth through murky dialogue. If you have something to tell me regarding Renford, then please do so. If not, then let us change the subject and continue our walk so I may enjoy my time outdoors."

He nodded and gestured for them to continue, but his silence was short-lived. "I hope that we're friends, Your Grace, even though we have not known each other long, and therefore I do not wish for what I'm about to say to upset you. I would never wish that," he said, reaching out and taking her hand.

Daphne swallowed the dread that rose in her throat. What did he know that he appeared so serious and grave? What had Renford done?

"But you will tell me in any case, will you not?" she said, knowing he would.

"All I shall say is that the duke seemed to have his hands full last evening, and that is not what you deserve as his new duchess. I know his reputation, you see, as I'm sure you do too. But even with all that said, that is not how one should treat a wife. Especially a duchess who's as beautiful and kind of heart as you."

CHAPTER
NINETEEN

Corey was going to pummel the little Frenchman to a pulp. He stood on the sidewalk, having been trying to catch up to Daphne when he noticed Monsieur Caddel making a direct path for her.

He stood and watched a moment, felt the trickling of anger run down his spine when the blaggard picked up her hand and placed it on his arm.

As if he had the right. Corey turned on his heel and returned home. He could wait to discuss the matter with Daphne when she returned from her outing.

Had she planned to meet Monsieur Caddel all along? Was there more to their friendship than she was leading him to believe? He made the steps of his house and paused, looking back in their direction. They continued to stroll farther away without a by your leave, and swallowing his annoyance, he left them to their devices.

"A missive arrived for you, Your Grace. I have placed it on your desk," Thomas said.

"Thank you." Corey moved toward the library. He shut the door and poured himself a large glass of whisky. It was early hours, yes, but after seeing Daphne on an enjoyable walk with another man, he needed a little pacifying liquid.

He slumped into his chair and broke the seal of the message. The heavy-stock paper, only used by the British Government, made the hairs on the back of his neck rise. Not that civilians would know such facts. Only those who had worked within their ranks, such as he, had.

> Renford,
>
> There are reports of a French spy circulating in London. You are receiving this message to notify you of such intelligence, and we would suggest you take this warning with great interest. The man in question is considered French, but may also be of Spanish heritage. Our report suggests the former and possibly a relative to the deceased Marquess William Laurier. Proceed with caution. Do not travel alone or unarmed. As per protocol, burn this missive upon completion of reading it.

Corey slumped back into his chair. He stared at the note for several minutes, taking in all that it said before he crumpled it in his hand and took it to the fire. Using a nearby candle, he lit the parchment and watched as it burned to ash in the grate.

A French spy in London? The thought unsettled him. Maybe he ought to return to Grand Oaks. He could control more who entered his lands and visited his estate. Here in London, anyone could come calling. It was no secret where the ducal Rendford residence was. It had been in the same location for hundreds of years. Anyone could assault them before they had taken two steps outside.

Daphne had never thought to stay in the first place. Had they not been caught, she would already be back in Grafton. Surely she would be fussed if they quit London and returned to Kent.

She had not seen her new home after all, and maybe it would be good for them to spend some time alone. He slept better in the country and wasn't plagued every night by nightmares. They might fight less over his rules if she was occupied by keeping the estate running as her position demanded of her.

He went back to his desk and sat. For several minutes he sipped his whisky, tapping the quill into the inkpot without using it. A thought so alarming in its possibility floated through his mind, and the tapping halted.

Monsieur Caddel.

French.

New to London.

He narrowed his eyes. Surely the spy would not dare to pretend to be part of the aristocracy. But then, a relative to William Laurier, whom he had killed, was part of old French nobility. Maybe they were related. It would certainly enable him to slide into the London *ton* without raising too many eyebrows. If one could talk and flatter as well as those in the upper ten thousand club, they would not be so difficult to fool.

Not even him, a spy himself.

Without delay, he stood and strode from the library. A footman stood to attention at his abrupt appearance. "Do not allow anyone to call as of today. We're not at home if anyone should ask. Please let the staff and Thomas know that we leave for Kent before the week is out," Renford ordered before leaving.

With long strides, he moved toward the front door, a footman quick enough to open it for him. He started back toward where he had seen Daphne last and could not see her in the distance.

She was nowhere in sight. He started along Mount Street, and not until he had rounded onto Berkeley square did he spy her at last. He skidded to a stop as a highly polished coach pulled up along Daphne and Monsieur Caddel.

With disbelief, he watched as she took the Frenchman's hand and climbed up into the vehicle.

"Daphne!" he shouted, hoping she would hear. She did not. But Corey got the distinct impression Monsieur Caddel had heard him. His smug, knowing smirk told him so before he joined his wife inside.

Renford started to run, heedless of what he looked like. A duke, a gentleman, chasing a carriage. But that carriage had his wife and one who, right at this moment, could be ensconced alone with a French spy. A man who wished him harm, no doubt, because of the harm Corey had done in France. But bedamned he would allow her to be hurt because of something he had done.

The carriage rolled forward, and no matter how much he tried to catch it, he could not close the distance between himself and the vehicle. He stopped and bent over, leaning on his thighs, and tried to catch his breath.

He would not allow himself to think the worst. Just because Monsieur Caddel was in London and French, that did not mean he was a French spy. There were several

Frenchmen in London who had traveled abroad, hoping to move forward from the war.

Even so, something about Monsieur Caddel did not sit right with Corey. Why was he so fixated on Daphne, for one? Was it because she was lovely, passionate, and amusing, or because she was Renford's wife?

If it was because of the latter, that meant only one thing. The French spy knew who he was and what part he played in the war. And that in itself was troubling.

Not just for today, but for both his and Daphne's future.

Daphne tried to relax and ignore that she ought not to be in a carriage with a man who was not her husband. But their discussion on the last book by Catherine Cuthbertson, *The Countercharm*, had morphed into an idea of visiting Hatchards to see what else was new to read. And so, here they both were, heading to the bookstore together.

Not that she would return home with Monsieur Caddel. That would never do at all, and she did not want to upset her husband any more than she already had this morning after their argument.

Unlikely, since you have other things to discuss with him.

One main discussion point was where he had been last evening and with whom. What was it that Monsieur Caddel had said? The duke seemed to have his hands full.

What did that mean? Nothing good in her estimation.

Daphne looked out the window as Monsieur Caddel rattled on about the genres of novels he enjoyed, but her mind wandered. Had Renford, but a week into their marriage, already had another warm his bed? Figuratively speaking, of course. She was certain that he had not come home with anyone, but had slept with them elsewhere.

Not that she would admit to waiting up to hear him return. Daphne inwardly sighed. She had not only stayed up but had listened out for any more nightmares he may endure after stumbling into his room at daybreak.

Why she cared, she could not fathom. She should not care at all. He was distant and cold one moment, but then, when they were alone, he was so much the opposite. All fire and light. Of good conversations and sweet gestures.

How could one man be so different within his one shell?

"Have I told you that you look quite fetching today, Your Grace? You take a man's breath away," Monsieur Caddel said, his voice lower than Daphne had ever heard it before.

She met Monsieur's eyes, not favoring the compliment, but deciding to make light of the situation instead of chastising him. "You ought to direct your flattery elsewhere, Monsieur. I'm afraid it is lost on me now," she said, hoping that would be the end of his attempt at flirtation.

"On the contrary, Your Grace. I always speak the truth, of that you can be sure, not just in flattery, but life in general," he explained.

Daphne threw him a cautious smile. Was he trying to tell her that what he viewed of the duke had been true last night? That Renford had been with another woman, and that is why he had his hands full?

Full of a whore's bounty.

Maybe even now, he was setting her up to be his mistress.

The bastard.

She bit the inside of her lip, forcing her eyes, which started to sting with tears, to cease leaking. She would not be a jealous fishwife. If he had a mistress, she would not die from the allocation. There were plenty of wives in London who suffered such fates.

She just did not want to be one ...

Daphne sighed and looked out the window, the idea of traveling to Hatchards no longer as promising as before. She did not want Renford to have a lover.

She wanted to be the only woman who warmed his bed. How could she earn his trust, his love, if they were not together? If he kept pushing her away and replacing her with nameless women, their marriage would fail, and she would have been better off letting scandal ruin her.

At least she could have returned to Grafton and lived out her days alone and without heartache.

"If you were my wife, Your Grace, I would never allow the melancholy that you look to be suffering right now to ever appear on your beautiful face. It is a crime to see that it is so," he said.

Daphne banged on the ceiling of the carriage, and it rocked to a halt.

"What are you doing, Your Grace?" Monsieur Caddel asked, his eyes wide with shock.

"Getting out," she said, opening the door and doing as she stated. "I forgot I have another appointment, Monsieur. Do forgive me. Good day." She strode back in the direction she came.

Back toward Renford, where he would not be allowed to push her away so easily. Not ever again.

TWENTY

Daphne returned home to find Renford pacing the library floor and all but wearing a mark on the Aubusson rug.

The sight of him disheveled, with a small sheen of sweat on his brow, gave her pause. Whatever was the matter with him?

"Renford?" she cautiously asked, remaining at the threshold.

He rounded on her, surprise and then relief crossing his features before his mouth thinned into a displeased line.

"Monsieur Caddel, Daphne? Is that who you'll make me a fool of with? I do not want you to see him again."

Daphne did not mind if she saw Monsieur Caddel again or not. But Renford giving out orders as if she were to obey them without a word as to why was another matter altogether.

She entered the room, strolled the bookcases, and pretended to seek out a tome to read. "You were spying on me?" she asked him.

He seemed taken aback by her question before he rallied and caught hold of his emotions. "I do not trust him, and we're not to entertain him until I know more of the man."

"You mean I'm not to entertain him, yet you can entertain yourself at all hours of the night. How was the gambling den, husband? Did you enjoy yourself?" she asked, wanting to know what he had been up to after leaving the house.

"How do you know where I was?" He narrowed his eyes before shaking his head. "Ah, yes, I remember. Monsieur Caddel saw me at Blackhaven's the other evening. I imagine he was only too delighted to tell you of my night. Embellish much, did he?" he asked her.

She crossed her arms and leaned against the bookcase, hating that he would mock her emotions. Make light of what he did as if that were nothing at all. Was the man really that cold? Did he have no heart at all?

"You seemed quite the popular duke from what I've heard. Your lap was occupied from all accounts."

"Was it now?" he stated. He started toward her, and the urge to flee burned strong in her blood. Daphne lifted her chin and stood her ground. She would not go. She had not been the one to do wrong, Renford had been, and he needed to explain himself.

"Monsieur Caddel is correct. I did have many ladies ply their trade before me."

The anger that simmered started to boil and was almost too much to bear. She clasped the bookcase behind her, forcing her hands not to scratch her husband's eyes out, that he dared even look at another woman.

Whether he wanted to be or not, he was her husband,

and she did not enjoy the thought of him being intimate with anyone else.

You do not love him. What does it matter?

She closed her eyes a moment, unsure if that was the case. Renford was a devastatingly handsome man. He had a dangerous air about him that made most women notice his presence. Not to mention his body was chiseled alongside the gods and his face made others pale in comparison.

But jealous? She would not be one of those wives who entered marriage with one understanding while all the time wishing for more.

You already wish for that.

She ignored her wayward thought, knowing he would not give her more. He had stated such himself, and she was being absurd to be angry at him for doing what he always said he would.

"Which one is your new mistress? Will you introduce us?" she asked, not hiding the sarcasm in her tone.

He chuckled, the sound deep and husky. The pit of her stomach clenched, and she swallowed, pressing farther into the bookcase when he came to stand at her front.

His arms reached about, pinning her against the bookcase. He chuckled, but the sound held no mirth. "Darling wife of mine. The only woman I want to fuck is you."

Daphne gaped, having not expected such a response. Did he truly mean what he said? Had nothing happened at all and was Monsieur Caddel putting her on edge for nothing?

The marriage, forced as it was, may have started under strained circumstances, but she did not want that to continue. She wanted a life with the man before her. They were married and had to try.

"So you didn't do anything with anyone else?" she

asked, fighting to hide the fact that the answer to her question could change everything for them both.

Should he be unfaithful, it would mean the end of any type of tranquil marriage or one that grew stronger with respect. All of that would be eliminated with one foul stroke of his infidelity.

"They tried," he admitted. "I gave them funds and sent them on their way."

Without warning, he picked her up and sat her on the bookcase shelf, stepping between her legs. He slipped her walking gown up over her knees, his large hands stroking her thighs.

Heat pooled at her core, and without being asked, she spread her legs wide for him. She met his gaze and reached for him.

They came together in a conflagration of desire. Their mouths fused, fought, and surrendered to each other. Their tongues twisted and teased.

Daphne moaned, reaching for his falls and ripping them open. Within several beats of her heart, he thrust into her, taking her, pushing into her while her back pressed against a mountain of books.

He worked her, took her, and owned every piece of her body. Daphne fought not to surrender, to give him absolute power over her senses, but there was no use. He merely had to look at her, want her in this way and she would go to him, surrender to him.

Give him all he wanted when he refused to do the same for her.

· · ·

Corey did not know what came over him, but he needed to have Daphne. He needed his wife to shatter in his arms merely to prove that she was well at home and with him again.

And not the man he suspected of being a French spy.

She fit him like a glove, took everything he gave her, and reveled in his touch.

Never in his life had one person occupied more space in his mind than the woman in his arms. He needed to protect her, keep her with him, safe from those that could do her harm.

"Come for me," he demanded, thrusting hard, taking her with relentless strokes. His balls tightened, and the pleasant ache that accompanied release teased his senses.

He was close, but she was closer, and he wanted to see her shatter in his arms. Come apart and give him what he wanted.

She writhed and arched her back. His hands explored her body, her breasts, her hips, her legs. He pressed his lips to the flesh on her neck and kissed the soft skin under her ear as his hands seduced her with novel pleasures.

Daphne nipped at his lips before taking his mouth in a searing kiss. She tasted as sweet as sin, like honey and cinnamon. She intoxicated him like no other, and his head swirled with each kiss. Deep and masculine grunts of pleasure, the petite sighs of the women, the wet slap of skin, and the creaking of the floorboards echoed in the room, swirled and mixed into the most pleasing sound he'd ever heard.

The first tremors of her orgasm convulsed about his cock and dragged him along to break when she did. He spilled his seed deep into her body. He may not be able to give her his heart, his secrets, but he could give her a future that was some of what she wanted.

"Corey," she screamed, her nails scoring his back as she worked against him, undulating and taking her fill of him. Satisfaction licked along his spine. He fought to control his breath, right himself, and return to earth. He could not get enough of Daphne. Why, even now, the sight of her disheveled hair, her cheeks pinkened with exertion, and her lips swollen from his kisses made him want her again.

Careful, Renford, or you'll fall for your own wife. A woman you never wanted.

Would that be so bad if he did? He could not change their lives now. It was set in stone, but that did not mean it had to be miserable or staid.

He could make her happy and satisfied in most ways. She just needed to become accustomed to remaining in her room in the dead of night.

Where it was safe.

Safe from him.

He met her eyes as she slowly regained her composure. Her legs dropped from about his hips, and she slid from the bookshelf. "Now, that is a much better way for us to start the day. Do you not think?" she asked him, a teasing grin on her lips.

He could not deny himself another taste of her and quickly brushed his lips against hers.

"Mmm, I do agree, Duchess. I shall darken your doorway each morning if you like?" he asked, hoping but not expecting to receive such advantages of being married.

"Perhaps," she said, pushing at his chest and brushing past him. "If you do not displease me by letting ladies of the night sit on your lap anymore. You're my husband, and only I have the right to be there."

The idea had merit, and his cock twitched. He could imagine her riding him while he sat, merely beholden to the wonderous, pleasurable ride. "I can agree to that," he said, not wanting the services of a mistress any longer in any case. Not when his wife was more than willing and capable of satisfying his every whim.

CHAPTER
TWENTY-ONE

The following afternoon Daphne sat in the drawing room, going through a multitude of invitations that had been sent to them in the morning mail, endeavoring to deduce which balls and dinners to go to the following week.

She had not seen Renford after dinner last evening. He had distanced himself yet again and retired to his library, citing paperwork as his excuse not to attend the Fairchild's ball.

Not that Daphne had felt like going in any case. Her body still hummed from their spontaneous lovemaking in the library, and she had not particularly wished to face Monsieur Caddel and explain her hasty departure.

She sat on the settee, and a small table sat before her. Laid out in date order were invitations they had received. There was more than one on certain nights, and it would be difficult to attend all of them, but she also didn't wish to offend anyone, especially as she was so new to the role of duchess.

"Ah, here you are," Renford said, striding into the room

and sitting next to her. He glanced at her invitations and waved a hand in their direction. "No need to bother with any more of those. We're off to Kent tomorrow. I have already informed your maid, and your trunks are being packed as we speak."

Daphne turned to face him, unsure if she should be pleased or uneasy about the turn of events. She supposed the London Season had never been something she aspired to attend, and she had only traveled a little in her nine and twenty years.

"Your estate in Kent, Grand Oaks? How long are we to stay?" she asked, thinking of all the responsibilities she would face there. She would have to meet the staff and pay a visit to the local village. Maybe there was a small parish school she could volunteer at. And if not, then there was always the possibility of starting one up to help the children.

"Until next year's Season. That is unless you become bored of Kent, and then we can travel to town. Or other places, if you would like. You only need to ask."

Travel? To other places? "Do you mean abroad, Your Grace?"

He pursed his lips, tipping his head to one side in thought. "Anywhere but France. I've had my fill of that country."

Daphne frowned, wondering why that would be so. "But you've been in Kent all these years. Why would you not wish to visit France?"

He cleared his throat, stalling. "I only meant, of course, I just do not wish to see any more Frenchmen than I need to right at this moment."

She watched him, unsure if she believed what he said

but willing to relent her curiosity. "Will it take us long to arrive at the estate?"

"We will change horses at numerous places along the road, but we will rest overnight at Tunbridge Wells and finish our journey the following day. We should arrive at Grand Oaks by luncheon, I should think."

"I'm looking forward to being back in the country. In fact, if we're to be there for some months, maybe I could find some occupation other than wife and duchess to keep me engaged," she suggested.

He leaned back on the settee and crossed his legs. He looked so informal yet so refined that he made her chest ache. She doubted she ever looked so. Certainly, before she became a duchess, she did not. Should she wear her country fashions in London, she was certain no one would ever speak to her again.

"What would you like to do?" he asked.

Daphne settled on the chair and faced him. "I want to help school children as I did in Grafton, the village where I lived."

"I know what village you lived in, Daphne," he said, his tone chiding.

She shrugged, uncertain most of the time what he listened to and what he did not. "I would like to do the same in Kent. Teaching letters and numbers gave me purpose, and I felt I was contributing something, helping the children better themselves. We could run it from the church, much as I did in Grafton. Would you mind if I sought such an occupation?" she asked, hoping he would not refuse her.

"I think it is a marvelous idea, and I know there is not one already in place. That the children will have lessons and be out from under their mother's skirts for a day, I should think will make you a most popular duchess."

Daphne chuckled, wishing they could always talk so and with such an easy conversation between them. He was so changeable that she was never sure what to expect from him from one day to another. Was he happy or wary? Seductive or suspicious?

"Thank you for your understanding, Your Grace. I'm now even more excited to see where you grew up."

"And I look forward to having you under Grand Oak's roof. All to myself without the distractions of the Season carrying you away."

Daphne inwardly sighed. Why could he not be so sweet and tender all the time? But, maybe when they were home, he would see that he could trust her, depend on her more than anyone else, and his bedroom rules denying her entry would be voided.

She could only hope that was the case.

He continued to stare at her, and something in his eyes made her forget about what they were discussing and shift to something much more enjoyable.

"You look as if you're thinking of things, Your Grace. Care to tell me what?" she boldly asked.

He glanced over his shoulder toward the door and spied a footman standing there. "Close the door, thank you," he ordered. A moment later, they were locked away in the drawing room.

Alone.

"I'm not thinking anything noble, Your Grace," he replied, pushing her back on the settee and moving between her legs. "And now you'll see what I mean by that."

. . .

Corey's mouth watered at the sight of his wife. She was utterly charming sitting in the drawing room, looking over invitations, biting her full lip while she thought about what events to attend.

For several moments he had stood at the threshold, watching her, simply enjoying the sight of Daphne.

She was so unaware of how beautiful she was. How charming and kind, even if she did at times argue with him.

"What are you doing?" She pushed his hands away from her gown he was busy hoisting toward her waist.

"I need to taste you," he said, waiting for her to either agree or deny his request.

Her eyes narrowed, but within a moment, she relaxed and lay back against the settee. He could not stop the grin that lifted his lips as he made himself comfortable.

"Just enjoy, Duchess," he said, parting her weeping flesh before kissing her in her most private places.

She pushed against his shoulders, and he relented, allowing her to gain a little control. "I cannot. This is too scandalous, even for you." She paused, biting her lip yet again. "Surely this cannot be possible or desired by you?"

He chuckled. "Oh, I want to. You have that wrong, my dear. Let me give you pleasure. You will not be disappointed. I promise," he hedged.

She relaxed yet again, and he went slower this time, running his tongue along her flesh, breathing in her scent, suckling her with restraint. It did not take her long to fall into a rhythm, to relax at his ministrations before she was writhing on the settee, heedless to who could hear.

Her sweet moans and sighs of delight filled the room, and he teased her flesh with relentless cadence. He pushed one, then two, fingers into her, and she shattered beneath him. Rode his fingers as if his cock were there instead. He suckled her, tasted her as she enjoyed the pleasure he bestowed.

"I need you, Corey. Please," she begged him.

He needed no further instruction. He ripped at his falls and came over her, joining her with a frenzied need. He fucked her, thrust into her, gave as much as she, and he came. Hard and fast in her willing cunny.

They lay entwined, breathless for several minutes before, with regret, he sat up and righted his clothes. He looked to Daphne, who did not move as fast as he, preferring to doze a little on the settee.

"You look utterly ruined and satisfied, and I must say, it is a pretty view indeed," he said.

She smiled and slowly sat up, slipping her gown about her legs as if they had not just fucked like two uncontrollable beasts. "I hope you come and seek me out on beautiful days such as this one when we're in Kent. I imagine I have a drawing room at Grand Oaks?" she asked teasingly.

"There are two drawing rooms, a ballroom, a library, dining, a conservatory, music, a gallery, multiple bedrooms, and nurseries. So many places that we can disappear to enjoy each other's company such as we just did." Already he wanted her, and he could not fathom it.

What made Daphne so different from every other woman he had ever been with? He knew the moment he had seen her at Dame Plaisir's ball that she drew him more than most, but why?

Maybe it was merely because she was his wife now, which changed things between them. Or he needed to get her out of London and safe in Kent, where no one came onto the grounds without him knowing it.

Maybe scandal or not, you would have married her anyway ... Maybe, wicked duke, you love her ...

The thought gave him pause, and he swallowed the panic that rose in his throat. Would he have? Did he love her? He glanced at Daphne, looking over her piles of invitations again, and could not imagine her marrying anyone else.

His hands fisted in his lap, and he took a calming breath, the idea of her sharing her bed, of giving her heart to anyone but him making his stomach churn.

CHAPTER
TWENTY-TWO

As planned, the following morning, they left early for Kent in the ducal carriage. Daphne had only had enough time to send off several letters to friends before she left, having decided to remain home last evening to ensure everything she would need in the country was packed.

The London town house was closed up, and it was not long before they made their way out to the waiting carriage waiting outside. Indoors, the servants threw dust sheets over furniture in preparation for their leaving.

The thought of traveling to Kent to see Renford's home, and now hers, left expectation to course through her, and she did not even mind the long carriage ride there, so excited was she to see her new home.

That the duke had given her permission to start a school for the local children meant she had much to keep her occupied when the duke was busy with estate affairs.

Renford helped her up into the carriage, and she settled her skirts on the seat, meeting his eyes and smiling when he settled across from her.

He was a tall man, and he stretched his long limbs, lounging against the squabs and reminding her of how he appeared yesterday when he visited her in the drawing room.

The thought of what they had done made heat thrum between her legs, and she could not help but wonder if such things were possible in carriages. They were seated, after all, and other than the fact they were moving, there was no reason why such pleasures could not be had.

Daphne fought to throw the wayward thought aside. She sounded like a woman who had become obsessed with her husband, which may be in a little way true. Last evening, when she was certain the staff was abed, she had slipped from her room, wanting to be with Renford, only to find his door was locked.

She had returned to her bed and had heard his nightmare start soon after and, this time did not try to help him. There was no use. He seemed determined to keep her at a distance, but surely there was a way she could support him. If only he would let her.

He yawned, and she smiled, looking out the window. She could only imagine his broken sleep after last night's terrors.

"How long before we're at the inn?" she asked.

"Five hours or so. We will arrive soon after lunch and rest for the afternoon. The journey to Grand Oaks is lengthier, and I do not think traveling at night is wise."

"Are there highwaymen down in Kent?" she asked, concerned by the idea. She had never seen one before, had never been unlucky in that respect, and nor did she want to be.

"Several have made their presence known, but during the day, they're normally still suffering the repercussions from their drunken ways the night before to mark us as a conquest. Even so, we have protection, both up on the box with the driver and in here. We are safe enough."

Not that Daphne doubted it. She knew no matter what Renford thought on the topic he would not do anything to hurt her and that he would keep her safe.

They traveled for some hours, and Daphne woke with a start when the carriage hit a particularly deep rut. She shuffled up on the seat and was pleased to see that Renford had, too, succumbed to sleep and had not seen her almost slip to the floor.

She peeked out the window, the sight far prettier than she expected. Rolling green hills, copses of trees, a little village far off in the distance. She wondered who lived there and how their lives were playing out.

Renford flinched, his boot hitting the carriage door. Daphne jumped and watched him for several moments to see if he settled. His face contorted into one of pure murderous rage and determination.

Unease settled in her stomach, and she thought as to what she could do. His warnings to her made her doubt her ability to reach him, to help him when he dreamed thus, but she had to try.

"Corey, I am here. You're dreaming." She wasn't sure if she ought to touch him. The last time she had done so, she had ended up with a knife against her neck. He kicked out and hit the door again, and she knew she had to do something.

She placed her hand on his leg but did not venture too close. "Corey, wake up. You're in a carriage on your way to Grand Oaks. Remember?" she said.

He jerked awake, his eyes confused and wide for a moment before he took a deep breath and seemed to remember where he was. He rubbed a hand over his face, sitting up, and she fought to keep the concern out of her tone. What had happened to him that he dreamed so awfully all the time? What was it that he was not telling her?

Did he have a traumatic event in his childhood? Or was he merely one of those unfortunate people that dreamed of chilling things?

"Will you not tell me why you have such trouble sleeping calmy?" she asked. "I promise I will not judge you if that is your concern. I merely wish to understand."

He looked out the window and gestured to a small cottage they passed. "Ah, we're here," he said, not answering her query at all.

Daphne looked out the window and saw the start of the small village. "This is Tunbridge Wells?" she asked. "I've never been so far south before." The little town seemed quite tidy, not to mention the houses appeared well kept, better than some back in Grafton.

"It is a busy village. A lot of the traffic from Hastings moves through here, so there is always trade and work to be had. It helps the people who live here to earn a good living."

"I wonder if they have a school?" she asked, wanting to lighten the mood.

Renford laughed and shrugged. "I should hope so. I think it would only improve everyone involved if they did."

The carriage turned into a yard before the Peacock Feather Inn. A delightful Tudor-style establishment with a courtyard that surrounded the building itself.

They were greeted by a stable lad, who helped with the door and steps before directing them to the entry.

Daphne had never stayed at an inn before, certainly not with a man. It was novel and quite odd being so far from anyone she knew with a man she had married but a sennight before, and now on her way to their future home.

The innkeeper, a sturdy, tall man who towered over both her and Renford, greeted them with a warm smile that seemed at odds with his hardened looks. She supposed men who worked in such conditions needed to be able to cease fisticuffs and arguments when they broke out.

Daphne glanced into the taproom and dining space a little farther away and noticed numerous people eating and talking, the fare smelling particularly enticing.

Her stomach chose that moment to rumble, and Renford glanced at her, grinning.

"We shall eat before going to our rooms. Bring us your best fare and two glasses of your best wine," he requested.

"Of course, Your Grace. I have kept your table free as usual when you travel through. I'll deliver the food myself," he said, pride beaming from the older man's features.

"Thank you," Renford said to him, taking Daphne's hand and leading her into the dining room.

As they rounded the corner, which gave them a better view of the space, Daphne could not believe that there was hardly a table free for anyone to use. Her stomach rumbled again, eager for the meal that was sure to be delicious. A place so popular was sure to be worth the wait.

They moved toward a table to the side of the room that overlooked the carriage yard. Renford helped her to her seat before taking his own.

"You prefer a view of the carriage yard to that of the town when you eat?" she asked, knowing she would prefer the latter.

"I like to see who is coming and going at all times. An old habit that is hard to break," he said, watching the yard.

And odd habit, she would wager. True to his word, the

innkeeper delivered several dishes for them to eat. Cheese and biscuits. Two soups that smelled of vegetable broth, and a pie and gravy to the side.

Daphne smiled, delighted by the fare. "Oh, my goodness, this looks wonderful, thank you," she proclaimed to the innkeeper.

"I'll fetch your drinks posthaste," he said, more than happy to serve them.

"This looks delicious." She picked up a spoon and tasted the soup. The flavor was unsurpassed, and dare she say it, better than their cook in London's ability.

"I know," he said, doing the same with his portions. "I stop here almost always on my way home. The accommodation is a little lacking, which you will see soon enough. Certainly not what a duchess is used to, but the fare is always fresh, and I've never come away feeling poorly."

"Always a good outcome," she said, laughing.

They ate in silence, the murmurings of other people as they enjoyed their food and spoke in hushed tones all that penetrated the silence.

"What the hell is he doing here?" Renford all but exclaimed. The distaste in his tone gaining several other guests' notice. "Now I know he's up to no good."

"Who is here?" Daphne asked, looking to the yard and unable to comprehend who stood talking to a carriage driver, completely unaware of who was watching him.

Monsieur Caddel.

TWENTY-THREE

aphne did not know why Monsieur Caddel was in the inn's yard, and nor could she understand why that infuriated Renford so much. "Do you think he knew we would be here?" Renford asked, but somehow Daphne did not think he was so much asking her but merely thinking aloud.

She watched Monsieur Caddel continue to speak and gesture madly about with the stable hand assisting him, and Daphne couldn't help but think that the Frenchman was upset about something.

"He looks annoyed," she observed, meeting Renford's gaze.

Renford's mouth pulled into a thin, displeased line before he stood and strode to the taproom. She heard him ask for their food to be sent to their room and something else in lowered tones she could not make out.

"Come," he said, returning to their table and glancing quickly out the window.

Monsieur Caddel was nowhere now to be seen.

"We're going to our rooms?" she asked, following

Renford, not daring to do otherwise. He all but vibrated with annoyance and eagerness to be gone.

A shame, for she was enjoying their meal together in the delightful dining space of the inn.

"Yes, I do not want to be interrupted by Monsieur Caddel yet again."

Daphne was unsure what he meant by that comment but did not think now was the time to ask him about it. They made their way up two flights of stairs and then along a narrow passageway. Their hastened steps atop the polished wooden floors all that broke the silence.

The innkeeper stopped before a door and, unlocking it, swung it wide. "Here ye are, Your Graces. Your preferred room."

The duke entered and looked around, even going so far as to check behind the privacy screen and one side of the bed. Was he looking for someone in their room? Daphne stepped into the space and placed her hands on her hips. What on earth was going on that she did not know about? This behavior was odd and uncalled for.

"Thank you," Renford said to the innkeeper. "And remember, we continued on. We're not staying here, as discussed. The carriage will need to be stowed where guests cannot see it and please inform the staff of my request."

"Of course, Your Grace. I will do all that you ask. You will not be disturbed."

The innkeeper closed the door, and Renford walked past Daphne and locked it. She rounded on him, wanting to know why he was so disturbed.

"What is happening, Renford? Why did we have to leave the dining room merely because Monsieur Caddel was in the inn's yard? You cannot think I'm the least interested in the gentleman besides being his friend."

He walked to the window and looked down, frowning. Daphne did the same and noticed Monsieur Caddel had finished speaking to the stable hand and was now talking to the innkeeper, who looked stoic and steadfast with his hands crossed against his sizable chest. If the Frenchman wanted to get anything out of the innkeeper, he did not look to be successful.

"There are things about me that you do not know. Things that could place you in danger, and there is a good chance that Monsieur Caddel befriending you has an ulterior motive."

"And?" she pushed, unwilling to have an answer that was no answer at all. He needed to tell her the truth, and he needed to tell her now. "I'm your wife, and while I know we do not know each other well, you must know that I would never break my oath to you in any way. I would never divulge anything that I should not to anyone. But if you do not tell me what I can and cannot talk about, how will I know if I'm doing the wrong thing?"

Renford moved away from the window and walked to the settee before the unlit hearth, slumping into it as if the weight of the world's problems were on his shoulders. "There is a possibility that Monsieur Caddel is a French spy and is here in England to do harm. Harm to myself, I should add."

Daphne's mouth gaped, and she fought not to exclaim that it could not be true. The war was over. Why would there even be a need for spies? But she did not. The consternation on Renford's visage gave her pause.

"How do you know this?" she asked, her stomach coiling in knots. Something was afoot with Renford, and although she did not know what it was, it would not be good.

"I cannot tell you that," he stated. "Just believe me when I say that I do not want to see you walking or getting into any more carriages with Monsieur Caddel from this day forward."

Daphne joined him at the hearth and sat across from him. "How did you know that I was with Monsieur Caddel? I did not divulge that information."

"I followed you after our row at breakfast and saw you. I tried to stop you, but you did not hear me."

Shame washed through her, and she wished she could go back to that day and not allow Monsieur Caddel to persuade her to join him at Hatchards. "I was not in the carriage long. I asked to be let out to return to you. We were going to the bookstore. Nothing else happened, I promise," she felt she needed to say.

His eyes narrowed on her, and he watched her in silence for several moments. When he looked at her like he was now, she could not help but feel he was trying to read her mind, think of all the possibilities as to why he ought not to trust her.

"All I can say, Daphne, is there are things in my past that could put you in harm's way. Please, if you're to go into the village, start working at the village church for your school or go for a ride, please let me know. I shall escort you or at the very least, ensure someone is with you at all times."

"I do not understand, Renford. How is it that you know there is a French spy, whomever that may be, is even here? Should that information be privy only to those who serve the British army?"

"As I said, please do not ask for more. I cannot tell you. I'm sorry."

Corey wanted to tell her. He wanted, if anything, to release the burden, even if it were the smallest amount, onto his wife. He had little doubt that Daphne could withstand the information and possibly do better with it than he was.

The people he killed haunted him at night, one man more than any other.

It was war, Renford. A situation of life and death. Either take a life or have your life taken.

All true, of course, but it did not help his conscience. He had not been born to kill. Hell, he had not even wanted to be a spy, but somehow that had materialized anyway, and now he would have to live with those consequences.

But the French spy in England, well, that was one complication he had not thought to arise. He already had so many to face during the dead of night when they attacked at his most vulnerable.

But if Monsieur Caddel was the French spy, and now he was here in Kent, following them to Grand Oaks, then he knew it had to be true. Not only did Monsieur Caddel know who he was, but what he did during the war.

And he wanted revenge on him for killing William Laurier.

"Tell me what I can do to make you feel better?" Daphne asked him, moving from her chair and boldly slipping onto his lap. She wrapped her arms around his neck and held him close. "You know that we're in the same room? That we'll be sleeping together tonight," she said.

"I shall sleep in the chair. You may have the bed," he stated.

A knock sounded on the door, and he lifted her in his arms, depositing her on the other side of the room, placing himself between her and the door.

"Come in," he barked.

A young maid entered with their tray of food, along with fresh beverages. "Your dinner, Your Graces," she said, dipping into a curtsy before leaving as quickly as she came.

Daphne moved past him and sat at the small, round table, dishing up their meals a second time. "I do not want you to sleep in the chair. Can you not try to sleep in the same bed as me? We have not yet as husband and wife."

He sat across from her and wished things could be different, but now that the French spy was following them, his nightmares had become more dark and violent, and he just could not trust himself. He would never forgive himself should he hurt her.

"I do not deny you to be cruel, Daphne." He reached out and slipped a stray curl that bounced against her cheek behind her ear. "I would sleep with you every night if I could. But I have already assaulted you once. I held a knife to your throat. I will not wake to your terror ever again."

"Is that not the risk I should take and choose for myself? You cannot protect me from everything. Not even yourself. I want to help you. Please, let us try. I want you in my bed."

Renford had never heard her state such a desire, and he could not deny that the more he spent with his wife, the more intoxicating she became. He did little but think about her, where she was, what she was up to, and with whom.

At least he would no longer have to worry about her being with that fiend Frenchman ever again.

He leaned back in the chair, pulling apart a piece of bread before stuffing a bite into his mouth. "Very well, one night. We shall try one night in the same bed, but I want you to take precautions in case I dream and do not know the difference between reality and fiction."

"Like what?" she asked.

He stood and went to one of their traveling trunks. He shuffled through his attire before he found what he wanted. "Like this small wooden mallet. Have it under your pillow or somewhere I do not know and if I try to hurt you, whack me a good one with it."

"You want me to bash you across the head?" she asked, her eyes wide with shock. "I cannot do that!"

"Yes, you can."

CHAPTER
TWENTY-FOUR

Daphne fought to hide the triumph that ran through her blood at Renford's concession. That he was to relent and allow her to sleep alongside him gave her some hope for their future. If she could prove to him that his nightmares could be shared, that she was there to help him, and that she was not afraid to try to assist him in overcoming this unseen trauma, maybe their union would thrive.

Should they continue to live separate lives, only coming together when their wants and needs became too great was not substantial enough to make a happy marriage. And she wanted her husband to love her. Her friend's marriages, all of theirs, were love matches, and she wanted nothing less with Renford.

Daphne went to her trunk, pulled out a clean shift for bed, and washed as best she could with the jug and bowl the innkeeper had left for them both.

"I can order a bath for you if you wish," Renford stated from the bed. He lay atop the bedding, his arm lazily behind his head as he watched her go about her nightly routine.

"A bath would be wonderful. I do feel a little dusty from our travels."

"I will ring the bell for a servant."

"There is a bell in here for such things?" she asked, looking about the room and spying the bellpull beside the fireplace she had not noticed before.

"This is, in essence, the ducal room I always use. Mr. Grant, the innkeeper, is a good man and accommodates most of what I ask for. A bellpull is one of them. Of course, when I've had house parties in the past, I always suggest that friends traveling from town use his inn before any others."

"A profitable union indeed then for him."

Within a minute, a servant came to ask what their query was before going to do as they requested. Daphne thought about bathing in front of the duke. They were married, after all, and it wasn't as if she had not done it before.

"You should bathe as well," she suggested. "I'm certain the tub will be big enough for us both. I do not think they will deliver a small hip bath for a duke."

He chuckled, reaching for his cravat that lay untied about his neck. He slid it free and threw it to the base of the bed, his eyes darkening with a hunger that made heat pool between her legs.

"Are you sure you would like that, Duchess?" he asked.

Before Daphne could answer, another knock on the door sounded. The duke got up quickly, not giving her a chance to do so. Two male servants stood on the threshold, holding the bath, which Daphne was happy to see would indeed fit them both.

"Besides, the fire will be fine," the duke ordered.

Not that a fire had been started, the evening warm

enough that they could open a window or two should they wish it and not catch a chill.

It did not take the staff long to fill the tub and supply two fresh linens and a soap that smelled of lavender before leaving them alone.

Daphne decided to be bold, wanting to prove to her husband and a little to herself that she was not scared. Not in any way.

She reached for the ties to her dress, thankful her maid had dressed her in a gown for travel that was easy to remove and one she could rid herself of alone.

Renford shut the door and slid the lock across. He turned and leaned against it, silently watching her, but she did not relent.

She watched him right back, wanting him to see that she enjoyed him as much as he enjoyed her and that she was there, willing to do whatever she could to make this marriage work.

Her gown slipped from her shoulders, pooling at her feet. Her stays were next, and before she could lose her nerve, she picked up the hem of her shift and slipped it over her head, throwing it aside.

A muscle worked in Renford's jaw, and an overwhelming feeling of power overcame her. He desired her. It was as obvious as her nakedness, not to mention his cock stood to attention, pressing against his breeches.

She kicked off her slippers. Bent over, slipping the silk stockings from her feet, and moved toward the bath of steaming, clean water.

Without waiting for him, she sank into the water, sighing at the pleasure of being clean and warm after a long day of travel.

Renford came up to the side of the tub, watching her

silently, and she waited for several beats of her racing heart to meet his eyes.

"Are you not joining me?" she asked.

He kneeled to the side of the tub, reaching for the lavender soap instead. "Let me wash you first, Your Grace. I think you need my ministrations," he murmured, his hands dipping beneath the water.

Daphne placed her hands on the side of the tub, leaning back, letting him do whatever he pleased.

"If it pleases, Your Grace," she replied, biting back her grin.

"It pleases me well."

Corey's cock ached in his breeches, but the sight of Daphne in the tub, the idea of touching her, washing her, learning more of her delicious body, was too much to refuse.

He lathered the soap, working it within his fingers. He picked up her toes, washing her feet with thoroughness and care. She chuckled, pulling her feet from his hold several times, but he would not relent.

"That tickles." She laughed, jumping as he worked the soap into her skin.

"Keep still, Duchess, or I'll never get you clean." He worked his way along her legs, washing close to her mons, but just shy of her cunny.

She watched him, her eyes growing heavy with need, and he knew that should he touch her there, she would be wet, ready as much as he was hot and rigid.

He washed her stomach, the undersides of her breasts, and her arms, and all the while, he could feel her annoyance grow. The little sighs, the small gasps when she thought he was about to give her what she wanted pushed him to taunt her more, work both her skin and need to a fever.

"Renford," she said when he paid particular attention to her hand for several minutes. "Get in the bath, husband," she ordered him.

His lips twitched, and although he would never tell her so, her ordering him about made him harder yet.

He stripped quickly, entering the tub without her having to order him twice. Water sloshed over the side, and she laughed, the sound carefree and untutored.

He pulled her into his arms, their bodies slippery from all the soap he had used to wash her.

She straddled his waist, wrapping her arms around his neck and wiggling on his lap, making herself comfortable.

"Now, this is much more preferable."

Corey couldn't agree more, and before he could utter a response, she reached between them, positioning him at her core and lowering onto his cock.

He moaned as her tight cunny wrapped about his staff. The room spun when she lifted herself, working him without any guidance or instruction.

He lay back and enjoyed her newfound freedom and audacity. She was marvelous. Her breasts rocked and swayed with her taking of him. His balls tightened, and he clasped her hips, bearing her deeper, harder in his ministrations.

"Oh yes, Corey," she moaned, her nails scoring the back of his neck. "You feel so good."

She felt phenomenal too. So damn perfect in his arms. The thought of not having her, of having some faceless mistress he would never feel anything for other than lust, paled in comparison to his wife.

How could he have thought that a mistress would have ever satisfied him? Everyone and everything dimmed compared to the lively, sweet woman he had been so fortunate to ruin in his arms. He would do anything to keep her safe, to make her as content as he could.

Tonight he would try to stay awake and keep her safe, but not before he had thoroughly made love to her.

Love?

The word reverberated about in his mind and made his world tip. He cared for her. Far more than he had ever thought he would. But here he was, a duke, one who had been determined to remain aloof from the fairer sex. Not marry and allow his ducal title to succumb to an unknown relative far down the ancestry line.

Instead, he had a wife, loving and caring in her ministrations to him. Far more than he deserved. She was too good for him, even with her common heritage. Still, she outranked him in all ways.

He had lied and killed, maybe to protect his country and countrymen, but it did not change his past. Nothing could do that, but she could change his future.

If he let her.

"Corey!"

He pumped into her as her first contractions hit, luring his body to join her in pleasure. He let go, spent with a cry of relief, and enjoyed the ride she brought them both.

She was perfect.

"Bed, husband?" she asked, slumping against his chest in exhaustion.

He needed no further prompting. He stood, lifting her from the tub with ease. He grabbed two linens lying nearby and dried them both before he threw her over his shoulder and walked her to the bed, dumping her unceremoniously onto the mattress.

She bounced, her eyes bright with merriment and expectation. "Bed will come, Duchess. But right now, I'm going to ensure you enjoy more of us."

She reached for him, pulling him down, and he went willingly. Gave himself over to his wife, her love and kindness.

He kissed her long and deep, wrapped her legs around his waist, and thrust into her.

And became one with his duchess.

TWENTY-FIVE

A whisper, then hushed, masculine words, woke Daphne with a start. She opened her eyes, strained to see into their room and make out what had woken her. Cold metal lifted her chin from the pillow as a dark shadow formed beside the bed.

They were not alone.

"Get up, Duchess. We have a score to settle," the voice of Monsieur Caddel whispered.

Daphne did as he asked, hoping and yet not hoping that Corey would wake up and save her. A score to settle? Whatever did he mean by that?

She left the bed and heard Corey shuffle and turn on his side, and she knew he did not know she had left. Should she scream? Would he shoot her now instead of later? The decision rendered her mute, and she crossed her arms over her chest, waiting on his next order.

He flicked his head near the door, and she noticed it stood ajar. How had he entered? She had seen Renford lock it herself. Daphne walked before him, heading toward the stairs. No doubt he wanted to leave, move her as far away from Renford as he could.

She stepped off the bottom steps of the inn and jumped back, gasping at the sight of the stable lad, throat cut and bleeding on the taproom floor.

Her body tremored, and she fought the urge to go to the boy to try to help him. At her hesitation, Monsieur Caddel pushed her past the young man and out into the carriage yard. "Get in," he ordered her, the cold barrel of the gun digging into her back.

"Where are you taking me?" she asked. Why was this happening? What was it that Renford was part of that meant Monsieur Caddel would steal her away in the middle of the night? She tripped on her shift and tumbled into the carriage. Scrambling to get onto her seat, she heard Monsieur Caddel order the driver north before joining her inside.

"Ah, here we are again. Alone in a carriage," he said as if nothing untoward was happening between them.

Daphne frowned and watched as the carriage rolled away from the inn into the inky black night. "You make light of this?" she queried, unable to fathom his amusement. "This is far from joyful, Monsieur Caddel. This is madness."

He scoffed, shrugging. "There is no merriment in what I have to do to you, Duchess. But my hurting you will hurt Renford, and that is all I care about."

"But why would you want to hurt Renford? He has done nothing to you," she said. There was something missing in this puzzle, and if she did not find out soon what it was that everyone kept from her, she would scream.

"He has taken everything from me!" Monsieur Caddel bellowed.

Daphne yelped, having not expected him to turn so raged so quickly. She huddled farther into the squabs and hoped that Corey had woken and was already looking for her.

Dear God, save her from this madman.

"Where are you taking me?" she asked.

"Back to London. I shall leave a stunning, dead surprise for Renford when he returns. Your house is closed up. The staff, as we speak, are on their way to Kent. You shall be nice and bloated by the time Renford arrives to save his loving duchess."

Daphne felt her mouth gape and her stomach churn at his words. Bloated? "Who are you?" she asked. He could at least tell her that, especially since he seemed determined to rid her of her life.

"Marquis Henri Laurier of Boulogne. But it is a title that should have gone to my elder brother, and would have, had your husband not put a bullet through his skull."

"Pardon?" she asked, gripping the seat as they rounded a corner far too fast. "We're being followed!" the driver yelled.

Caddel's eyes went wide, and he looked out the window, numerous French and English curses flying off into the air.

"Keep going. Hold your pace," Monsieur Caddel ordered before grinning at Daphne.

"Your husband, the esteemed Duke of Renford, is a murderer. A hired killer for the British army. A lowly spy that is not fit to lick my boots. My brother was merely one of many whom your husband slaughtered." Monsieur Caddel met her eyes and smirked. "How does the duke sleep at night? Well, Your Grace?" he queried.

Daphne swallowed, unable to comprehend what

Monsieur Caddel was saying. Was it true? She supposed it was, but if he worked for the British army, then he was under orders. How could Renford be blamed for that?

Was that why he did not sleep well at night? Out of guilt?

She closed her eyes a moment, wishing she could comfort him, tell him she knew his secret and why he was haunted.

Her poor love.

Love?

She watched Monsieur Caddel settle himself on the seat as if they were about to play an excellent game. The man was mad, had wiggled his way into being her friend, and all the while so he could act out this revengeful plan.

"Do you think your brother would approve of this?" she asked. "He was a French officer, I presume, working under your army's code of conduct. Kill or be killed or something along those lines. War is never fair on either side. But this, what you're doing is revenge killing. A death you want merely to soothe your cruel wants and needs. There is no honor in that."

"Shut your mouth, Duchess, before I put a bullet between your pretty, white teeth."

Daphne did as he asked. Something about his cold, life-less eyes that shone back at her in the shadowed carriage told her he would do as he threatened.

The carriage continued to barrel along the road, barely slowing for turns and ruts, and several times she almost lost her seat. And then she heard him.

Renford.

Her eyes met Monsieur Caddel's, and she knew he was already aware the duke was chasing them.

"Ah, he's come to play," he said, pausing. "I will give

him credit. The man did not take long to learn you were no longer beside him."

As much as it shouldn't, Monsieur Caddel's words warmed her. Corey was coming after her. He would not let this madman harm her in any way, nor would she allow him to take away the one man who had captured her heart.

Her husband.

"But then, when a pretty, succulent woman such as yourself is sleeping next to a man, there would be few who would not want to sample your charms."

Monsieur Caddel's gaze turned lascivious, and a chilling shiver ran down her spine. He moved to sit beside her, and she scurried to the opposite seat. But before she could halt him, he clasped her about the waist, leaping against her back and pushing her facedown onto the squabs.

Daphne screamed, the cool night air kissing the backs of her legs as he hoisted up her gown. She tried to roll away, shuffle to the floor, but he was too strong, too determined to hold her still.

"Stop, Henri. Please stop," she begged.

The driver yelled out instructions, and the carriage started to slow.

"Keep going, you fool," Monsieur Caddel hollered, the sound of her gown ripping as he fought to lift it above her bottom.

Panic seized her, and for a moment, she thought she might be sick. Out of the corner of her eye, she spied the flintlock lying on the seat, and without hesitation, she picked it up, but before she could aim it at Monsieur Caddel, the gun went off, firing forward in the carriage.

The moment the shot rang out, the carriage lurched. Daphne screamed and clasped the chair as best she could before the sensation of floating overcame her. She did not remember anymore after that, nothing but blackness, merely the blissful safety of the dark.

C orey watched with horror as the driver of the carriage fell onto the road. His horse jumped the man's moaning form and continued on, pushing his mount harder to reach the carriage. But it was too late. The horses, with no driver to guide them, bolted around a corner. The carriage tipped and then flipped several times, rolling between trees, only coming to a stop against a large boulder.

He wrenched his horse to a stop and dismounted, running for the carriage without heed. Panic assailed him. Was Daphne dead? Had he lost the one woman whom he had grown to care for? The thought almost buckled his knees. He ran past Monsieur Caddel, thrown from the vehicle, who lay near one of the wheels that still spun from the impact.

"Daphne!" he shouted, climbing up onto the vehicle and forcing the door to open. He spied her then, lying against the opposite door, her brow bleeding from a large gash, her eyes closed.

He made his way to her and hoped she lived. He reached for her and touched her cheek. She did not move, did not make a sound, and his stomach revolted at the idea that she had died. That his past had stripped her of her future.

"Daphne," he said again, leaning down and listening for her breath. For several moments he heard nothing, and then she murmured the softest word, but the best he'd ever heard in his life. His name.

"Corey?" she asked, her eyes fluttering open.

"Daphne," he breathed, wanting to wrench her into his arms but thinking better of it. "Can you move? Do you think you can climb out? We must leave," he said, hoping she would agree.

She held on to him, pulling herself up, and relief swamped his bones, making his legs feel weak.

"I think I can climb out." She winced when she stood, clasping her brow. Pulling her hand away she noticed it was covered with bright-red blood, and her face paled. "I'm bleeding," she yelped, meeting his eye.

"I know, love. But I'll have you back at Tunbridge Wells soon, and all will be well. You'll be safe." She had to be. There was no other choice for him now. Had not been a choice for him in truth since the night he met her at Dame Plaisir's ball.

His virtuous beauty come to save him.

TWENTY-SIX

Corey jumped from the carriage and turned to help Daphne down. She went into his arms willingly, and he held her a moment, holding her close and thanking God she had lived.

He could have lost her. The thought was as revolting as Monsieur Caddel using her to get to him. The bastard ought to have acted like a man and faced him head-on. Not use his wife.

"Do not think you're getting out of this so easily," a hoarse voice said from behind.

Corey turned and scanned the road and surrounding trees. Where he had stepped over the Frenchman, he was no longer lying. And then he spied him, leaning against the base of an elm, one arm clearly broken from the peculiar angle it sat, the other shaking as he aimed the flintlock toward them.

"His real name is Henri. William Laurier's brother, Corey. Said that you killed his brother in France."

Corey cringed, remembering the bastard well and glad he had killed him. The man was cruel and did unspeakable things to both the French and English during the war, men and women alike. He had no preference. He had not deserved to live. That his brother would seek revenge was not a threat he had thought to face. No sane soldier would act out in this manner.

"You're going to shoot us?" Corey stated, wondering if he could talk some sense into Monsieur Caddel, Henri, or whomever the man was. "Our countries were at war. I was under orders just as your brother was. Had he won that day, I would have died. I was just fortunate enough to shoot first."

"You shot him in the back of the head. He didn't even have a chance to fight you, you weak bastard."

"Your brother was a killer, and a good one. If I had not caught him unawares as I had, he would have killed me without balking. Your brother was better at what he did than I. Any soldier in my position would have done the same." At least, that was what Corey told himself, but he, too, had doubts. Hearing them from Henri, calling him out for the way he had taken Laurier that night in Paris, haunted him. To shoot anyone when their back was turned was not noble.

The tentative touch of Daphne, reaching for his hand, calmed him. "You did the right thing, Corey. I'm glad you did, for if you hadn't, I would never have met you."

He turned, knowing that if this was their final few moments together, he wanted to look at her, not the unhinged Frenchman against the tree.

"You know what I did? Who I was?" he asked.

She nodded. "I do, and I think it's noble. You fought for England. You fought to keep people like myself safe. Placed yourself in situations that most of us would run screaming from. I think you're a hero." She leaned up and kissed him, and he held her tight. He was no hero, not by far, but her understanding went so far in believing in them and their future. If they were to have one after tonight.

A shot rang out, the crack piercing the quiet night. Daphne stumbled back, falling to the ground before Renford knew what had happened. She clasped her arm and screamed, and realization struck.

Corey rushed to her, seeing her perfect, unblemished skin he had marveled at only weeks ago, was now sliced open by a bullet, bleeding down her arm and onto her hand. He inspected the wound quickly, thanking whoever listened that it was only a graze and not life-threatening.

"He shot me." Her eyes went wide, and he could see she did not understand what had happened or why. A rage unlike any he had ever known came over him, and he left Daphne, knowing he could not allow Henri to shoot a second shot.

The blaggard fumbled to reload the flintlock, but he wouldn't manage it. Corey hoisted him off the ground, the gun dropping at their feet, and he stared at him for several moments. "Unlike your brother, Henri, I will look into your eyes as you take your last breath," he said, snapping the man's neck before he could protest.

He had not wanted to do that in front of Daphne, but the man was crazed, determined on revenge, and she would never be safe, any children they had and himself, had he not done what he must.

Corey left and returned to Daphne, ripping a portion of his shirt and tying it about her arm.

"It hurts," she cried, tears streaming down her face. The sight lodged a lump in his throat, and he scooped her up in his arms, carrying her to his horse.

"We are not far from Tunbridge Wells. You will soon be

tended to by a doctor and given a tincture. You'll feel better soon, darling," he soothed.

She threw him a loopy smile, and he wondered if she was about to swoon. "You called me darling," she mentioned, her eyes brightening at the notation.

He chuckled. How was it that this was what she noticed right at this moment? She had been shot, after all. Should she not be more concerned with her injury than what endearments he used?

"You are my darling wife. My love," he tested, having never said the word to anyone before in his life.

She sniffed, reaching for him as best she could. "I love you too, Corey. So much that even when you infuriate me, and I want to strangle you, I also want to hold you, love you as you deserve."

"I do not deserve you. For years I believed I did not deserve such affection, not after all I had done during the war. I've taken so many lives, Daphne. How many of those had loved ones? Sweethearts, just like you? Mothers and fathers who mourned their passing." He shook his head, uncertain still. "I have nightmares about them all. In my dreams, I relive those moments of the war, and I cannot seem to rid myself of them. That night when I held the knife to your neck, it was not you beneath me, but another long gone from this earth. I do not trust myself," he admitted, having never told anyone of his troubles before.

"You were a soldier, a spy, and under orders, Corey. You are not responsible for doing what you were commanded to do. And you do deserve to be happy, and I intend to make you so for the rest of our lives." Daphne held him, and he wrapped himself around her, hoping that was true, that he would not be so guilt-ridden as he was for the rest of his days. "I will be by your side, and we will conquer these ghosts and finally lay them to rest."

"I love you so much," he admitted. "I tried not to. I tried to keep you away, push you back each time you moved a little too close to my heart, but it was no use. You lodged yourself there nonetheless, and now I cannot imagine a life without you. I cannot promise that what I've done in the past will not come for us again. I cannot promise my dreams will not haunt me if we share a bed. But I need you. I do not want to drive you away anymore. I love you, Daph," he said.

Tears streamed down his wife's face, and he wiped them away, kissing her. She kissed him back through tears, a promise, a declaration. A new start for them.

From this day forward.

EPILOGUE

Grand Oaks, several weeks later

Daphne heard the steady beat of Corey's heart under her cheek, and for a time, she lay against his chest, marveling at how far they had come.

It had been several weeks since that terrible night at Tunbridge Wells. A night she could have lost her life or that of her dear husband, whom she fell more and more in love with every day.

She slid her hand across his chest, circling his nipple with her finger and counting the seconds until her touch roused him.

"Hmmm, wife, what are you doing?" he asked, rolling her onto her back and settling between her legs. His cock, hard and ready, teased her, slipping against her in the most delicious way.

She chuckled, slipping her ankles about his back and hooking them above his bottom. A very lovely bottom, too, that she could now admire as much as she wanted since they shared the ducal suite at Grand Oaks and her husband had taken to sleeping naked every night.

"Another night, my love," he stated, pride and a tidbit of relief in his tone.

She ran her fingers through his ruffled hair, wanting to see his handsome face. "Yes, another one without a night-mare. It's been six weeks since you had a bad dream. Let's hope that they will cease forever."

His cock pressed against her mons, and she wiggled beneath him, her core aching and wet. They had taken to waking up just so, in each other's arms, and she never wanted it to change.

"Let us not jinx ourselves, but quietly hope."

She nodded, lifting off the bed a little and placing him at her core. His eyes darkened with hunger, and without further prompting, he slid into her, taking and filling her with his manhood.

She loved that he fit her so well and felt so good. Soothed the ache, the need whenever they came together.

"What a delicious way to wake in the morning." He took her lips in a searing kiss. Their bodies came alive, sought, and gave all that they had. Daphne moaned and arched her back, seeking him deeper, harder.

He did not disappoint. He thrust into her with maddening strokes. Filled and inflamed her, pushed her toward the pinnacle of pleasure she had come to crave.

She would never get enough of Corey.

"You are everything to me." He bit her neck, suckling her skin before whispering in her ear words that no duke ought to know, nevertheless say to a woman.

She shivered. "You are wicked, duke," she teased.

He met her eyes, his heavy with desire. "Come," he said, thrusting into her. "Come, my darling wife."

She needed no further urging. She came hard and long, the pleasurable sensations coursing through her quim, out to every part of her body to the very tips of her fingers and toes.

"Corey," she moaned, rolling her hips and seeking all she could from him.

"Daphne," he panted, his liquid warmth spilling deep inside. She watched him. Reveling in the pleasure, the ecstasy that settled on his features.

How she loved him so very much. "I love you," she said, clasping his face, reveling in the happy life they had created together. The intoxicating nights and sweet days with so many more to come.

"I adore you," he said. "And I love you too."

Daphne reached for him, kissing him soundly.

Before he rolled her onto her front and showed her just how wicked the Duke of Renford really was.

Dame Plaisir's would be proud.

Dear Reader,

Thank you for taking the time to read *Wicked In My Bed*! I hope you enjoyed the tenth and final book in my The Wayward Woodvilles series!

I'm so thankful for my readers and their support of this series. If you're able, I would appreciate an honest review of *Wicked In My Bed*. As they say, feed an author, leave a review!

Alternatively, you can keep in contact with me by visiting my website, subscribing to my newsletter or following me online. You can contact me at www.-tamaragill.com.

Tamara Gill

DON'T MISS TAMARA'S OTHER ROMANCE SERIES

The Wayward Yorks

A Wager with a Duke

My Reformed Rogue

Wild, Wild, Duke

The Wayward Woodvilles

A Duke of a Time

On a Wild Duke Chase

Speak of the Duke

Every Duke has a Silver Lining

One Day my Duke Will Come

Surrender to the Duke

My Reckless Earl

Brazen Rogue

The Notorious Lord Sin

Wicked in My Bed

Royal House of Atharia

To Dream of You

A Royal Proposition

Forever My Princess

League of Unweddable Gentlemen

Tempt Me, Your Grace

Hellion at Heart

Dare to be Scandalous

To Be Wicked With You

Kiss Me, Duke

The Marquess is Mine

Kiss the Wallflower

A Midsummer Kiss

A Kiss at Mistletoe

A Kiss in Spring

To Fall For a Kiss

A Duke's Wild Kiss

To Kiss a Highland Rose

Lords of London

To Bedevil a Duke

To Madden a Marquess

To Tempt an Earl

To Vex a Viscount

To Dare a Duchess

To Marry a Marchioness

To Marry a Rogue

Only an Earl Will Do

Only a Duke Will Do

Only a Viscount Will Do

Only a Marquess Will Do

Only a Lady Will Do

A Time Traveler's Highland Love

To Conquer a Scot

To Save a Savage Scot

To Win a Highland Scot

A Stolen Season

A Stolen Season

A Stolen Season: Bath

A Stolen Season: London

Scandalous London

A Gentleman's Promise

A Captain's Order

A Marriage Made in Mayfair

High Seas & High Stakes

His Lady Smuggler

Her Gentleman Pirate

A Wallflower's Christmas Wreath

Daughters Of The Gods

Banished

Guardian

Fallen

Stand Alone Books

About the Author

Tamara is an Australian author who grew up in an old mining town in country South Australia, where her love of history was founded. So much so, she made her darling husband travel to the UK for their honeymoon, where she dragged him from one historical monument and castle to another.

A mother of three, her two little gentlemen in the making, a future lady (she hopes) keep her busy in the real world, but whenever she gets a moment's peace she loves to write romance novels in an array of genres, including regency, medieval and time travel.

Made in the USA
Las Vegas, NV
04 April 2024